"I know what you'

"Doing?" Tony a

"I don't need a
don't need a babysitt

"What do you need, Jess?"

Seductive, laden with invitation, the words hung between them like steam rising from her coffee cup. She raised her eyes to his, telling herself she was prepared for his playful grin, and that in the sparkling light of morning she could handle it.

But he wasn't grinning. And his look wasn't playful.

"What do you need, Jess? Tell me and it's yours. . . ."

WHAT ARE *LOVESWEPT* ROMANCES?

They are stories of true romance and touching emotion. We believe those two very important ingredients are constants in our highly sensual and very believable stories in the LOVE-SWEPT line. Our goal is to give you, the reader, stories of consistently high quality that may sometimes make you laugh, sometimes make you cry, but are always fresh and creative and contain many delightful surprises within their pages.

Most romance fans read an enormous number of books. Those they truly love, they keep. Others may be traded with friends and soon forgotten. We hope that each LOVESWEPT romance will be a treasure—a "keeper." We will always try to publish

LOVE STORIES YOU'LL NEVER FORGET
BY AUTHORS YOU'LL ALWAYS REMEMBER

The Editors

INTO THE
NIGHT

CINDY
GERARD

BANTAM BOOKS
NEW YORK · TORONTO · LONDON · SYDNEY · AUCKLAND

INTO THE NIGHT
A Bantam Book / September 1994

If you would be interested in receiving protective vinyl covers for your Loveswept books, please write to this address for information:

Loveswept
Bantam Books
P.O. Box 985
Hicksville, NY 11802

ISBN 0-553-44299-6

Published simultaneously in the United States and Canada

Bantam Books are published by Bantam Books, a division of Bantam Doubleday Dell Publishing Group, Inc. Its trademark, consisting of the words "Bantam Books" and the portrayal of a rooster, is Registered in U.S. Patent and Trademark Office and in other countries. Marca Registrada. Bantam Books, 1540 Broadway, New York, New York 10036.

PRINTED IN THE UNITED STATES OF AMERICA
OPM   0 9 8 7 6 5 4 3 2 1

To my husband, Tom,
who once got me out of the rain
with an offer even more compelling than pizza.

My thanks to 96.5 FM radio
for opening their doors
and letting me in.
Special thanks to Carla Tollefson
for her expertise, her warm smile,
and her wonderful voice, which intrigued me to
the point of making a radio personality
the heroine of this story.

ONE

The world was full of heroes. So where were they when she needed them? She wasn't greedy. She'd settle for one. One single, solitary hero. In a DeSoto from Tijuana. She wasn't picky either. If he had a potbelly and a bald spot, she was his if he'd just get her out of this blessed rain!

Head down, shoulders hunched against the downpour, Jessie Fox kissed the prospect of a rescue and her sweet disposition good-bye as she slogged through the mucky, wet grass along the side of the freeway. So much for Big Al's Garage and his "Satisfaction Guaranteed Is Our Motto." Al could take his guarantee along with her reconditioned carburetor and put it where the sun don't shine. Which, she acknowledged as she dragged a heavy fall of wet hair out of her eyes, was exactly where she was—stalled in the dark on I-8 without a dry spot or a hero in sight.

The traffic shot by her. All these cars, and not

one person could find it in himself to stop. Welcome to friendly southern California, she thought bleakly. She considered screaming in frustration, but she was too weary to make the effort. Not just because of her car and the mess it had left her in but because of all the changes in the last year. The strain of coping made her feel more vulnerable than was warranted and more self-pitying than she'd ever allowed—even during the divorce.

"Buck up, Fox," she lectured herself. "You made the right move. It's a good job. A great opportunity."

And tonight and a few other minor incidents notwithstanding, great things had happened to her since she'd uprooted herself from Kansas City three months earlier.

San Diego for instance. Now, there was a real plus. She loved San Diego, the color, the ocean, and usually the weather, she reminded herself as she skidded through a puddle and narrowly avoided landing face first in the mud. She still missed the Midwest, but Sarah was here. Being close to her daughter took the edge off Jessie's occasional pangs of homesickness.

Her heart softened, as it always did, when she thought of Sarah. Yes, being close to her was great, even though her independent little coed sometimes didn't see it that way.

Once more with feeling, Jessie rallied as the wind picked up and pelted rain full into her face. It was great being in San Diego. It was just that with her jacket and jeans taking on water weight like a leaky boat and her feet sinking into mucky clay, it was a bit of a stretch to gain the upper hand over pessimism.

"An aging accountant with a rash," she muttered as she plodded on. Any hero in a pinch, and this had gone long past pinching. She was wet. She was cold. She was tired. And she was so anchored in her misery that at first she didn't notice the vehicle that had pulled into the breakdown lane, slowed to a crawl, and begun keeping pace beside her.

With a grateful, sidelong glance Jessie sized up the car—which wasn't really a car. It wasn't really a truck either. It could once have been a van, she decided, then quickly recatalogued it as a relic from the flower-child generation that had mated with an urban assault vehicle. It was also just cause to reconsider the "any port in a storm" philosophy she'd been spouting since she'd abandoned hope and the dry interior of her car about a mile back.

Without breaking stride she checked out the overextended axles that set a black chassis three feet above the river running along the pavement. The rusted-out body had been painted by an artist who had clearly been in the midst of an identity crisis, and depicted a veritable weed garden of psychedelic flowers that vined from hood to doors and mingled indiscriminately with shooting orange flames. Shocking-yellow letters declared PEACE—a concept that more than one other vehicle had taken exception to, if the dings and dents along the body were any indication.

By California standards it probably wasn't all that

unusual. Her midwestern background, however, couldn't quite come to terms with it. She couldn't stall a shiver, this one as much from apprehension as from cold.

When one final glance confirmed that the dark silhouette behind the wheel could not possibly belong to a woman, she decided that being wet wasn't as rankling a notion as it had been a few minutes ago. And, she realized with considerable relief, she was more discriminating about her rescuer than she'd originally thought. Clothes might make the man, but his mode of transportation spoke volumes about his character. Even though she couldn't make out the features of her prospective "hero," she'd pass this time, thank you very much.

"It's not getting any drier out there," a deep voice rumbled through the rain.

Now, there was a news flash. A regular Einstein had been dispatched to save her. Einstein in the van from hell.

"I'm fine," she said, even as she flirted with the notion that there was something familiar about his voice—something teasing and taunting that sent a tune of recognition humming through her senses.

She chalked off that possibility to hysterical hope. Between the traffic noises, Michael Bolton's raspy rendition of "Georgia" wailing from the van's radio, and the rush of rain-soaked wind whipping against her face, she could hardly recognize her own voice, let alone get a bead on his.

A very real fear teamed up with that niggling recognition, however, when she recalled the eerie phone call she'd fielded on the radio station's request line last week. That call was still too vivid in her mind. That call had had her looking over her shoulder ever since and stepping up her pace right now.

When he matched her speed, she gave a dismissive wave of her hand, motioning him away.

Just enjoying a walk in the rain, her suddenly springy steps implied. Yeah, right. Pneumonia wasn't an idea she'd like to cozy up to, but neither was the prospect of being tomorrow morning's lead news story: "Local radio celebrity, Jessie Fox, of the Falcon and the Fox late-night duo, was found murdered near her abandoned car on I-8 early this morning."

Another violent shiver, triggered by that thought, had her clenching her jaw to keep her teeth from chattering. More determined than ever to take her chances with the rain, she waved him on again.

"Thanks just the same. There's a station up ahead," she added for emphasis, and prayed he'd take the hint and move on.

He didn't. She tried to ignore the squeal triggered by complaining brakes. When the passenger door swung open with a serrated creak and a sinister invitation, however, she stopped in her tracks. Her heart kept right on chugging.

Compelled by a riveting combination of curiosity and fear, she squinted into the dimly lit interior of the van. Muzzy shadows and an overall impression of size and strength didn't do much to slow down the trip-hammer beat of her heart. She couldn't see his face from this angle, but what she could see sent another shiver rippling down her spine.

The shoulders and chest filling out a black V-neck sweater were both broad and solid. The arms visible beneath the sleeves he'd pushed up to mid-forearm were toned and tan. A swirl of dark chest hair peeked out of the V-neckline, and the column of his throat was drawn from lines both sinewy and strong.

No ninety-pound weakling here. And no chance of holding her own if he decided to do things "his way."

No doubt about it, Jessie told herself, she should be running, not gawking. Yet she stood there, her eyes wide open and her mouth pinched shut.

"For Pete's sake," he muttered. "This is ridiculous. Would you just get in?"

Even through the rain and traffic noise, his tone implied that his was the voice of reason.

Despite her doubts, she grappled with that persistent impression that she knew more about him than she was able to piece together.

Still, she declined with a hesitant "I don't think so."

"Suit yourself . . . but I've got pizza."

Pizza? She was going to be lured to Lord only knew what kind of fate by the promise of pizza?

No sooner had that incredible thought settled than a few brain synapses snapped together and made a connection with the resonant timbre of that voice.

She dragged her sodden hair out of her eyes and bent down for a better look.

Eyes as black as midnight and just as mysterious stared back at her from a face shrouded in shadows and a curtain of rain. They were dark, dangerous eyes that glinted in amusement . . . and familiar invitation. Still, it wasn't until he shifted behind the wheel to fully face her and the glare of headlights from an oncoming car set a flash of silver shimmering at the hollow of his throat—an artfully molded falcon suspended from a silver chain—that the believer in her KO'd the doubting Thomas.

She almost laughed with relief.

God was good. Even if he did have a warped sense of humor.

It was the falcon she recognized, just as she finally recognized the smile of the man who wore it. Only one man she knew had a smile like that, encompassing, inviting, flirting yet guileless. Sinful yet sweet.

Tony Falcone.

While Tony Falcone wasn't a stranger posing a threat of the unknown, he still represented a threat. At least he did to her. It just wasn't the kind she'd expected to find in a strange vehicle on a dark and rainy night.

Instead this was a man who, without realizing it, without even trying, presented another kind of hazard. Hard as it was to admit it, he was a real and serious risk to her better judgment. He had been ever since he'd hired her three months ago.

With a deep sigh and a muttered "Why me,

Lord?" she grudgingly admired the ironic twist fate had managed to arrange that night. It didn't mean, however, she was going to let him see how he affected her.

She met his gaze and aimed for light and snappy. "Did you say pizza?"

His smile spread full face when he realized she'd tuned in to who he was. "Um-hmm. Double cheese. Spicy sausage."

She pretended to consider. "Momma Leone's?"

His dark eyes danced. "Is there another kind?"

Two things happened to her then. Despite her water-soaked skin she felt her cheeks flush with heat. Inside her rain-soaked clothes her insides melted to mush. It was those kinds of reactions to his sexy smile and devil-without-a-care arrogance that constantly gave her so much trouble.

Daily she fought to control her response to him. To date she'd been successful. At least she thought she had. And just because she was doused in mud and rain and a heavy coat of vulnerability didn't mean she could afford to let that response get the best of her now.

Giving in to necessity, and determined to show at least as much maturity as Sarah, she climbed up into the passenger seat.

"I don't suppose there's a prayer that pizza isn't smothered in anchovies," she said, tugging the door closed behind her.

"Hey . . ." He affected an affronted scowl. "What's a pizza without anchovies?"

"Good?" she suggested, and allowed him an indulgent chuckle.

Feeling marginally more in control now that she was out of the rain, she peeled off her soaked jacket and tossed it into the back of the van. She made a mistake then. She shot him a sidelong glance that got stalled by the sculpted, angular beauty of his profile —a reaction she was sure he was aware of and had experienced far too often for his own good.

She wasn't up to this tonight, she decided, sighing in defeat. He was just too darn much man. His flashing eyes and the thick fringe of lashes surrounding them were as dark as his hair. Lush and full-bodied, with a hint of curl, his hair had stopped being respectable about four inches ago, although she had to admit the ponytail he sometimes pulled it back into looked right on him.

What wasn't right was that ever since she'd posed with him for that darn billboard to promote their radio program, she'd had to double her efforts to keep from wondering what his hair would feel like between her fingers, tickling her skin.

She was hopeless, Jessie decided. As rotten as her luck was, her timing was even worse. Forty-two, she was coming to realize, was a bad age to be without a man. Her hormones had reached an unprecedented zenith. At least that seemed to be the case whenever her new boss was around. Nothing since puberty and pregnancy had been as hard on her as Tony Falcone. Even Helen Gurley Brown hadn't prepared her for the things this man did to her pulse rate.

"So . . ." Still looking entirely too amused, and entirely too handsome, Tony checked the traffic in his rearview mirror, then pulled out into it. "What's a nice girl like you doing out in a rain like this?"

She snorted and looked away. "You actually use that line?"

"And do you usually climb into strange vehicles?"

Concentrating on the wipers' rhythmic sweep of the windshield, she tried not to visualize another half grin forming, a grin that would emphasize the deep dents in his cheeks and define the cleft in his chin.

"Only in extenuating circumstances," she said with what she hoped came across as throwaway banter.

"Which includes monsoon rains?"

She nodded toward the pizza. "And offers of food."

He chuckled again. "And here I thought food was supposed to be the way to a *man's* heart."

"I never did understand that cliché." Wrapping her arms around her waist, she marveled at the steadiness of her voice and the stupidity of this conversation. Chalking it up to an increasing sexual awareness that nearly had a stranglehold on her better sense, she settled deeper into the seat and hoped for the best. "Most men I know couldn't care less about eating. It's more of a biological necessity and a nuisance for them. Whereas most women would bargain with the devil for a decent quiche."

"That may be true . . ."

He paused. The silence that followed extended an

invitation to her to face him again. Fool that she was, she accepted.

Big mistake number two. Her breath stalled as she watched his gaze slide in a leisurely caress across the wet cotton T-shirt clinging to her breasts. He took his sweet time about it, lingering on her nipples, which were hardened by wet and cold and—thanks to his smoky appraisal—by a latent, unbidden arousal.

"That may be true, Jess," he repeated softly, "but don't discount all aspects of a man's appetite."

As if the suggestion in his words and shimmering in his eyes weren't enough, he leveled her with a devastating though playful wink. "Once we take care of your appetite, we'll see what we can do about taking care of mine. My place or yours, *Foxie*," he added, his eyebrows waggling in a comically suggestive leer that, thank the Lord, accomplished two purposes. It snapped the sexual tension and put things back in perspective.

This was something she could deal with. Tony Falcone wasn't experiencing any of the problems she was with libido. He was just being his usual teasing self: the innocuous flirt whose advances she couldn't possibly take seriously, because he didn't take himself seriously.

Flirting was simply Tony's style. He loved women. He loved making them laugh, turning their hearts to pudding, and lifting their spirits with his warm glances and winning grins.

Just her luck, he was darn good at it. Her only consolation was that the dreamy looks and wistful sighs that followed Tony around the station were an indication that she wasn't the only woman suffering from the same type of dementia.

"You can take me anyplace," she finally responded, "as long as it's warm and dry. But don't get the idea that it makes us even, Falcone. You may have gotten me out of the rain, but I'm still trying to decide if I'm grateful or mad as hell."

"Mad?" He braked at a light and flashed her a look full of engaging innocence and irritating irresistibility. "What'd I do?"

"You let me stand out there in that mess for five minutes more than I should have, that's what you did." She was feeling more and more in control as she worked up a show of anger. She had a right to be a little on edge, a little wired. He'd scared her half to death before she'd figured out who he was. "You let me think you were sizing me up for assault and battery, *that's* what you did. Why didn't you tell me it was you in this . . . this monstrosity?"

"Well, it wasn't like you could get any wetter."

She gave an unladylike "Hurmph."

"Hey, I'm sorry," he said, sounding genuinely contrite.

The sincerity in his expression sent another shiver rippling through her.

"Honest, Jess. I didn't give it a thought that you wouldn't recognize me. And then when I realized you didn't, I couldn't resist teasing. Just a little. Ah, come on. You looked so cute—"

Her low growl cut him off.

"Now what?"

She sliced him a warning glare. "*Cute*, Falcone?"

He laughed. "So what's wrong with cute?"

"Nothing." She hated the sniping sound of her voice, but used it to her advantage as a defense to fight the attraction. "Nothing is wrong with *cute* . . . if I were twenty. And perky. And a cheerleader. But I happen to be forty-two, the *mother* of a perky twenty-year-old cheerleader. And cute does not cut it for me anymore. Cute, quite frankly, smacks of patronization. Cute—"

"Okay. Okay." One broad palm patted the air in supplication. "I stand corrected. Lord, don't make it into a platform. I was just making conversation. Trying, even, to pay you a compliment. Touchy. Touchy."

Touchy and out of her ever-loving mind. She did not want to deal with what she'd just said. Did not want to puzzle out why she'd felt the need to drive home the fact that she was the forty-two-year-old mother of a twenty-year-old. He knew that. He'd met Sarah when she'd dropped into the station one day to say hello.

Besides, it wasn't as if a thirty-something man needed to be warned away from a forty-something woman. She eyed him covertly and shuddered again. If his thirty-fifth birthday had come and gone, she'd take a bite out of her carburetor before she shoved it down Big Al's throat. Her delinquent hormones notwithstanding, she didn't want him to be interested anyway.

She hung her head and hoped that, like a bad cold, these feelings would pass. She should be remembering who she was with too. One did not willingly tick off one's employer unless another fantastic job offer loomed on the horizon.

She sucked in her breath as a runnel of cold water trickled down her back. "You're right. I'm sorry. I should be thanking you for the rescue, not biting your head off."

After all, he had gotten her out of the rain. He'd turned the heater on full blast too. It was working hard at warming the cool, clammy air to snug, hothouse levels. If she hadn't been chilled to the bone and fighting off a bad case of crankiness, she might have been a little more gracious.

"So, what happened out there anyway?" he asked.

Compelled by nerves as much as by the need to be distracted from his overwhelming presence, she told him how she'd ended up stalled on the freeway.

Sarah had wanted to borrow Jessie's laptop computer to finish a paper due on Monday. Since Jessie had wanted to pick up a paperback to get her through the night anyway, she'd run the computer over to the campus. Simple really. Just her luck she was going to end up with another garage bill, a pair of ruined Nikes, and bronchial pneumonia as an added bonus.

The book had better be good.

Sarah's paper had better get an A.

She huddled deeper into the seat. "How did you know it was me—or were you just out trolling for damsels in distress and figured you'd gotten lucky?"

He angled into the far-right lane, headed down the next exit ramp, and gave back as good as he got. "Gave up trolling last week. I'm into luring now. Glad to see the pizza works."

She rolled her eyes.

"I recognized your car, Ms. Fox," he explained easily. "While little white compacts are a dime a dozen, not many have ninety-six-point-five FM bumper stickers and Missouri license plates that spell out FOXIE. Stood to reason that the poor soul walking would be you."

The poor soul shivered and sent a silent thanks to Sarah for the vanity license plates she'd given her mother for Christmas.

Tony shot her a concerned look. "We need to get you warm and dry. You get to shivering much harder, you're going to shimmy us right off the road. Hold on. I don't live far from here."

"At this point one more revolution of the tires seems far from here," she muttered. In an effort to take her mind off how cold she was, she checked out the van's interior, which was distinguished by yards of zebra-striped fun fur and glow-in-the-dark stickers of everything from Barney the Dinosaur to Bon Jovi.

She made a mental comparison to the classy black Lexus that occupied Tony's parking space at the radio station. "I'm not surprised to see you have a second vehicle," she managed to say, even though her teeth had become bent on chattering. "But s-s-somehow, I figured you for something a little more understated."

A streetlight illuminated another slashing smile. "Prom night."

Prom night? "Oh. Well. That explains it, then."

His grin was positively devastating. "My nephew had a hot date. I let him believe he was doing me a favor by letting me borrow his wheels tonight. Use of my car was his payback."

She could have done without another reminder that in addition to being poster-perfect gorgeous, Tony was also a nice guy. Only a nice guy would manipulate someone into thinking he was doing something for the nice guy, when in fact it was the other way around. She worked hard at ignoring that particularly endearing trait.

"You think this"—she paused, taking an expansive look around her—"this *vehicle* will make it as far as your apartment?"

"No worries," he assured her. "According to Jared, this is the bitchinest machine east of the San Andreas fault."

"Why don't I find that analogy comforting?"

He laughed again. The sound was cream rich and honey sweet, and penetrated her bloodstream like a straight shot of smooth Canadian whiskey.

How, she wondered, could she feel so hot and so cold at the same time? Hugging herself, she tried to take comfort in a small but very real probability: Much more of Mr. Falcone's brand of heat and her clothes would dry from the inside out.

TWO

Good to his word, and not a moment too soon, Tony pulled into a driveway five minutes after he exited the freeway. He didn't live in an apartment, though, as Jessie had suspected. He lived in the Singing Hills, in a rambling ranch house set in the midst of golf-course green grass and a plant-studded yard. The huge lot, bordered by a hedge of oleander and a wealth of flowering jacaranda trees, overlooked the lights of El Cajon nestled in the valley below.

After a rumbling and screechy stop, Tony set the brake and turned off the ignition.

Jessie just sat and stared for a moment, having trouble taking in this scene of domestic tranquillity.

"Something wrong?" he asked.

"No, I . . ." She stopped and offered a lame smile. "I guess I was expecting . . . I don't know. Maybe a high-rise downtown? At the very least a condo on the beach," she added as he helped her out of the van.

"Yeah, well, it just goes to show you," he said as he snagged his mail from the mailbox, then led her under a latticed patio roof to his back door. "You don't really know me very well, do you?"

That evidently was a major-league understatement, Jessie decided as he steered her inside. He waited for her to toe off her wet shoes, then ushered her through the kitchen, down a long hall, and into a spacious bedroom decorated in subtle shades of jade, silver, and mauve.

"There's a heavy terry robe in the closet and a bath across the hall. Do I have to coax you to take advantage of both?"

"No, sir," she answered gratefully, and with a cold and shaking hand opened the closet door.

"Use all the hot water you need and anything else that comes in handy." He stopped on his way out of the bedroom and turned back to her. "Just toss your clothes in the dryer—first door on your left. I'll warm up the pizza.

"And, no," he added when she started to protest, "it's no trouble. I'm hungry, and there's more than enough for two. After we get you dry and fed, we'll figure out what to do about your car."

Her car. She'd almost forgotten about her car. She'd like to forget about it, but forced herself not to, figuring a healthy shot of anger would help warm her up. But when she stepped into the shower, naked and shivering, it wasn't her car that came to mind. It was

Tony, and how much nicer it would be to have him making her warm again.

Groaning at the utter desperation that thought suggested, she ducked her head under the steaming spray and waited for the water to wash away her chill.

"If you had stuck with the job you'd been hired to do, you wouldn't be having these problems," she muttered to herself as she reached for the soap.

"But no. You weren't happy tucked in your own little office by yourself just writing copy anymore . . . something you're darn good at too." The collection of Addy Awards given by the advertising industry and the four Merits of Excellence filling wall and shelf space in her office proved that. "You had to go for the glory."

For eighteen years she'd worked behind the scenes at KCMO in Kansas City. That was what Tony had hired her to do at KXAL. The lure of not only writing commercial jingles but providing the voice that uttered the finished product, however, had been too much to resist when he had offered the opportunity shortly after she'd started working there.

She should have resisted, though, because one thing had led to another, and now her whole career —not to mention her emotional equilibrium—had altered drastically.

"It was the Fat Man's fault," she decided, rinsing off and then squeezing shampoo into her palm.

If the Fat Man hadn't gotten laryngitis, Tony wouldn't have asked her to fill in for the ailing DJ on the late-night request line two months ago. If he hadn't gotten laryngitis, Tony wouldn't have dropped into the on-air studio to help her over any rough spots she might have running the radio board.

If the Fat Man hadn't gotten laryngitis, she continued, working the shampoo into a frothy lather, Tony wouldn't have hung around and indulged a whim to share some impromptu "air chatter" with her to set her at ease.

Darn that Fat Man. Because of him, that particular show had fielded the most phone calls the station had ever received. As a result, "Into the Night with the Falcon and the Fox" was now a Monday-, Wednesday-, and Friday-night feature every week.

Well, it was too late for muttered misgivings now. She'd gotten herself into it, and it didn't look as though there was any way out of the situation at this late date. If the continuing phone calls were any indication, the show's popularity had elevated the two of them to local celebrity status.

The notoriety she could live with. In fact she secretly enjoyed it. Plus she'd found out she was an "on air" kind of person. She liked the spontaneity, the adrenaline rush of beating the clock and keeping things flowing. She liked the challenge of orchestrating a smoothly running program, segueing with increasing skill from one mix to another and keeping the show tight.

What she didn't like, what was giving her so much trouble, was the intentional implication that a romance existed between her and Tony.

"What's the harm?" Tony had asked, shrugging

off her concern. "So we play on the angle that they think we're romantically involved. Everybody loves the idea of a romance."

Apparently everybody loved the idea of *their* romance. Thanks to Tony's special type of playful, suggestive banter, he had perpetuated that notion but good.

Jessie was handling that too—as long as Tony sat on one side of the radio board and she sat on the other. But that stupid billboard he'd talked her into posing for had taken things too far.

More than anything else, that billboard had added to the sexual excitement she felt whenever she was around him.

It had to have been Scarlett and Rhett, hadn't it? It had to have involved a sensuous satin gown, searing looks, and a steamy clinch that had been shot over and over, until she'd been more aware of him as a man than any woman should ever be without benefit of a bed.

She rinsed away all traces of shampoo, wishing she could do the same with the memories that welled up of being held in his arms. Wishing for a return to the level of maturity she'd prided herself in possessing but that an abundance of overactive hormones seemed to have leached away.

"An accountant would have been a lot less trouble," she mumbled as she shut off the water and stepped out of the shower stall.

While Jessie showered, Tony headed for the living room. After laying out kindling in the fireplace, he set a match to the dry tinder, then watched while the flames caught hold. After adding more wood, he roused himself and sized up the room. Except for the scattered mess of several days' newspapers, which he gathered and tossed into the emptiest magazine rack, things were in pretty good shape.

Tut, stretched regally across the back of the low-slung leather sofa, watched him with judgmental calm through eyes of cool topaz.

"It'll do," he assured the Siamese after a final scan of the room.

In the kitchen he found a beer in the fridge and slipped the pizza into the oven to reheat. Taking a chance that Jessie would prefer wine, he snagged a corkscrew, selected a bottle of burgundy from the rack, and opened it.

"For the lady," he explained to Tut as the big tomcat sidled around the corner, tail and chin cocked in a fashion befitting his kingly name.

"And for you," Tony added as he poured a generous portion of cat food into Tut's bowl.

Beer in hand, he walked across the kitchen, braced his free hand above his head on the patio doorframe, and contemplated the rain—and the woman currently occupying his shower.

What was it about Jessie Fox that had kept her lingering on the edges of his thoughts since the day he'd hired her three months ago?

It wasn't that she was an exceptional beauty,

though Lord knew, she definitely encouraged a second look. What she was, he decided, thinking back to his first impression, when she'd stepped into his office for her interview, was pretty. Pretty in an all-American, fresh-faced, woman-with-integrity-and-grit way. But he'd hired her on the basis of her résumé and her experience. And he admired her for her ability, which she'd shown on a daily basis was apt and professional.

Interesting, then, he thought as he watched the lights of El Cajon winking through the rain-streaked glass, that it wasn't her ability that he thought of most often when he thought of her. And though he hadn't admitted it to himself until that moment, since they'd done the photo shoot for the billboard, he thought of her too often.

Even more interesting was how she'd ended up in his house that night.

He took a long pull on his beer, not wanting to think about what could have happened to her if he hadn't been the one to find her walking. Stalling that thought, he went to the phone and made a quick call to arrange for her car to be picked up. He'd just cradled the receiver when the soft pad of bare feet on polished oak floor brought his head around—and his blood to a slow, heavy stall.

"Thanks." She nodded toward the phone, indicating she'd overheard the conversation.

"No problem. Stan's a friend of mine."

"Well, I guess it's my good luck you've got a friend with a tow truck."

"And my good luck that I found you before someone else did."

Their eyes met and held, telegraphing what they were both thinking: The huskiness in his voice had placed more than a casual emphasis on his words. He'd heard it, and he knew she had too. Her eyes gave away her surprise. For Tony the intimacy of both the thought and the moment held far too much appeal. As did Jessie Fox.

She looked hot-water flushed, comfortably lost in the folds of his white terry robe, and as softly sexy as any woman he'd ever seen. Knowing there was nothing but dewy pink skin and gently sloping curves beneath that robe hit him hard, right where it hurt.

He fought the effects of a slow arousal as the scent of his soap drifted around her like a misty, seductive cloud. It was a masculine scent that shouldn't have smelled feminine. On Jessie, however, it did. Feminine and sensual and as alluring as the hesitant look in her eyes.

It occurred to him then that the capable, self-assured, take-charge woman he'd hired was exhibiting an arresting amount of vulnerability. She tried to hide it, but it showed anyway. To know that beneath all that cool control beat the heart of a woman not entirely sure of her own appeal, proved an intriguing puzzle.

It made him wonder if her ex had done a number on her. In a flash of unsolicited anger, he wished he'd had an opportunity to bang the jerk's soft head against a hard wall.

His instantaneous reaction would have amused him if it hadn't been so strong. As it was, it took him by surprise. So did his preoccupation with Jessie.

He wasn't looking for a relationship. At least not anything serious. His life was full and rich without one. In the category of "the good life," his settled right up there at the top. He came from an affluent family and was carving out his own successes, both financial and personal. In most books he lived the quintessential American dream—an easy southern California lifestyle and a rewarding career.

When it came to women, he'd never lacked for company. And he'd never been attracted to older women. Against all odds, though, and in spite of the denials he'd been fabricating since day one, Jessie was proving to be the exception.

Her vulnerability touched him. Her soft gray eyes enticed him. And her voice, a seductive blend of smoke and honey and substance, just plain turned him on. It made him think of sultry nights; long, lazy loving; whispered requests; and shimmering responses.

He swallowed hard, then reached around her for the wine he'd poured earlier.

"Feeling better?" he asked, too aware of the tingling contact as their fingers brushed when she took the wineglass from his hand.

"Much better. Thank you." She smiled tentatively, snuggled deeper into the robe, and sipped. "For the wine and the warmth."

Her gaze held his for a seeking moment before she shifted her attention to the window.

It had been only a moment of contact, but it had been charged with awareness. A sizzling sexual awareness that left him wondering and wandering deeper into territory he had no business exploring. *What would it be like to take her to bed?*

Off limits, Falcone, he reminded himself firmly. It went against the grain and against policy to mix business with pleasure. When he'd taken over at KXAL four years ago, he'd installed hard-and-fast rules, including no office romances. Personally they were not to his liking or taste. Further, defending even a suggestion of sexual harassment could stress the radio station's legal budget and make a difference between a year that promised to take a major bite out of the debit column and one that took it deeper into red ink.

But seeing the way Jessie's slender body sweetly filled his robe had him questioning why in the hell he'd ever made that particular rule. Also edging into his thoughts was the reminder that for as long as he could remember, he'd bent the hell out of most rules anyway.

"This song keeps running through my mind . . ."

Her smoky voice brought him back to the moment; her soft smile drew him back into her eyes.

"Something about 'it never rains in southern California.' "

He smiled. "Another illusion shattered." He

tipped up his beer and wished he could find it in himself to drag his gaze away before she accused him of staring. "We call it June gloom. It came a bit early this year, but in a few weeks it'll be over and you'll forget you ever saw anything but sun."

A small tremor ran through her. A leftover chill from her excursion in the rain, he wondered, or an involuntary reaction to the looks that were passing between them? Either way he was spellbound as she drew the robe's lapels tighter to her chin. He watched her profile as she sipped her wine, her full lips lingering on the rim of the glass . . . and he thought about the way they'd feel feathering across his body.

Her chestnut-colored hair was shoulder length, thick, and still a bit damp. The weight and the sheen of it put him in mind of heavy satin and sleek moon-kissed silk. And like the whisper of her mouth across his body, he imagined it drifting across his skin.

Unwisely he moved a step closer, unable to fight the effects of yet another small intimacy. One that proved exceedingly erotic. Just as her skin was scented with his soap, so was her hair scented with his shampoo.

"Your hair is still wet." He reached out to touch it, then checked himself at the last moment, knuckling under to the wisdom of restraint. It was one thing to play fast and loose on late-night radio for an audience speculating about a romance between them. That was business. That was revenue. It was another to hear the hushed sexual awareness in his tone and realize he was playing to an audience of two. And to wonder when he had stopped thinking of it as playing.

Abruptly he turned toward the stove. "Why don't you head back into the living room. I lit a fire. Get comfortable. Get warm. I'll be right behind you with the pizza."

Just as soon as he got his head screwed back on straight, he promised himself, then swore under his breath when he became fascinated by the gentle sway of her hips as she walked away.

What the hell was happening here?

Jessie perched uneasily on the end of Tony's sofa. She stared into the fire and tried to talk her way around the suggestions she'd seen in his eyes. But with his robe wrapped around her, his scent woven into its threads to tease her senses, it was too difficult to explain her impressions away.

For a moment, as they'd stood side by side in his kitchen watching the rain, she'd sensed a sexual energy that wasn't entirely one-sided. In that moment she'd been certain she wasn't the only one fighting the attraction.

Granted it had been a long time since she'd fielded a sensual invitation from a man. So maybe she'd been mistaken. Maybe it was a combination of the dark, rainy night, the intimacy suggested by the two of them alone together, and a little wishful thinking. *Misplaced* wishful thinking.

She had to have read his signals wrong. After all, she was out of practice. Practice? She smiled grimly. Until the divorce a little over a year ago, she'd been out of circulation.

Sometimes she still had to stop and put that little piece of reality into focus. Almost twenty-two years of what she'd thought was a comfortable, happy marriage had ended one bright May morning when David had calmly, if remorsefully, announced over his coffee that he had filed for divorce.

It wasn't that he didn't love her, he'd assured her. He simply wasn't *in* love with her anymore. She'd just sat there, shocked, her heart pounding, aware of every tick of the clock on the wall, of every toast crumb lying under her fingertips on the breakfast table, of every note as the birds sang outside in tribute to the beautiful spring morning, as if her world hadn't just fallen apart.

It wasn't her fault, he'd offered generously. She understood, didn't she? Couldn't she at least try to understand? He didn't want to hurt her. But he wanted—actually he *needed*—to get out of the marriage while he still had a chance to make a new relationship work.

Well, far be it from Jessie not to comply with one of David's needs. She'd dedicated twenty-plus years to doing just that. She hadn't seen any point in changing course then.

Even though her heart had been breaking.

Even though her pride had been ripped to shreds.

For Sarah's sake, for the sake of her own sanity,

she'd agreed to everything David had wanted. And then she'd prayed that he'd come to his senses and come back to her.

Denying a pain too sharp to deal with, she'd existed on that hope by insisting she was fine. She'd managed to fool even herself for a full three months after he'd left.

She hadn't been fine, though. She'd been dying inside. The day Sarah had come home and found her huddled in the corner of the kitchen, racked with uncontrollable sobs, was the day she finally realized she had to get on with her life. Not just for her own sake but for her daughter's.

The hell with David, she'd told herself. If he didn't know when he had a good thing going, then he didn't deserve her. She'd quit loving him that day. She'd quit hating him too. From that point on she had just felt a hollow ache for everything he'd thrown away.

Her thoughts turned, as they often did, to Steven —kind, patient Steven Hall—and another kind of ache gnawed, reminding her of what *she* had thrown away when she'd left Kansas City. Steven had been such a good friend during the divorce and after. More than that, he'd wanted to marry her. She had hurt him badly when she'd told him no.

It was days like these, when everything went wrong, that the memory of Steven's solid, steady strength had her second-guessing her decision. While it had been some time since she'd heard from him, the last time he'd called he'd made sure she knew his offer was still open.

She frowned into her glass of wine. Maybe friendship was as good a foundation as any to base a marriage on.

"Is it the prospect of the anchovies or my company that's prompting that look?"

She glanced up at the sound of Tony's voice. Judging by his concerned scowl, her thoughts must have been reflected on her face.

One hand balancing two plates and the pizza, the other juggling the bottle of wine and his beer, he waited, uncertain, in the middle of the room. His hesitance was completely at odds with an innate confidence she suspected was rarely shaken. For some reason she was touched that it was shaken now.

"Actually neither." She forced a smile. "I was just thinking about how I ended up here."

One corner of his mouth quirked up. "I think it had something to do with a faulty carburetor."

"There is that." Rising, she relieved him of the pizza, setting it on the end table beside the sofa. "But I wasn't referring to *here* specifically tonight, as in on your sofa." *And in your robe*, she added silently, then wondered if she'd telegraphed her thoughts again when his gaze locked on hers.

Wrapping the robe tighter around her, she sat back down and tucked her bare feet up beside her hips. "I was referring to San Diego. The station. The job."

"Must be the fire," he said, easing down to the

floor and stretching his legs out in front of him. After handing her a piece of pizza and getting one for himself, he leaned back against the sofa, crossed his ankles, and balanced the plate on his lap. "It's a good place for reflecting. But now that you mention it, how did you end up in San Diego? I've wondered the same thing now and again."

She looked down at him, contemplating his definition of *now and again*, before deciding she'd been too busy examining ulterior meanings that night.

The simple truth was he was her boss and he'd offered her a kindness. They were sharing a pizza while she dried out. *In front of his fire. In his robe. Surrounded by the scent of soap and musk and man that all combined to make her think of uncommon intimacies and hot, steamy sex.*

Stifling a groan, she concentrated on picking off anchovies and prayed to God she wasn't turning into a pathetic cliché of the sex-starved divorcée.

Resolved to straighten up and deal with this hormonal ambush later, she steered herself to level ground.

"I'm sorry," she said, embarrassed when she realized the silence had lapsed for several moments. "I'm a little preoccupied tonight. We were talking about . . ."

"San Diego." He twisted at the waist, hooking an arm on the cushion by her knees, and looked up at her. Though his eyes relayed his curiosity about where her thoughts had been, he didn't press it. "You were about to tell me how you ended up in San Diego."

"Right." She drew a fortifying breath. "The fact of the matter is the job was the deciding factor. I needed a change. Coincidentally you offered one. Pretty simple really."

He angled her a look. "Really?"

She shifted uncomfortably, then decided what the heck. He wanted honesty? She'd deliver. "I had a good job at KCMO. I liked it. I wrote good copy for eighteen years. And Kansas City had always been home. But . . ." She hesitated, then took the leap. "After the divorce I realized that in addition to a change of pace, I also needed a change of scene."

A minute passed before his voice broke the silence. "Too many bad memories?"

She looked from the fire to her wine and finally to him. "Too many good ones."

His eyes, so warm, so expressive, so intent on her, glittered darkly. "His loss."

She thanked him with a small, tight smile that told them both she was still fighting to believe her next statement. "Yeah. That's kind of the way I've got it figured."

For too long their eyes held, and questioned, and explored. For too long she felt the pull that could only lead to trouble tug against the need to maintain a steady course. In the end it was Tony who finally broke contact.

Dragging his gaze away from hers, he concentrated alternately on his beer, the pizza, and the fire, before he spoke again.

"It's odd, isn't it?" he began thoughtfully, still staring at the fire, still stretched out in that lazy sprawl that defined the long, muscled legs inside his jeans.

"What's odd?"

He shrugged. "It just occurs to me that for all we've seen of each other the past few months at work, I know very little about you. Do you find that at all ironic, given the premise for the show and the time we spend together in the studio?"

"Oh, well, that's show biz," she said lightly.

"Speaking of show business . . ." He turned back to her, a smile flirting with the corner of his mouth. "What do you think of the billboard?"

Jessie grimaced. She'd been wondering when they were going to get around to talking about "the billboard." It had just gone up that week on Mission Gorge Road. She didn't *want* to talk about it, because she'd decided it was the real culprit for all these sexual overtones and undercurrents.

"I think," she said carefully, "I'm going to live to regret the day I ever agreed to do that shoot. No, wait. Make that past tense. I *have* lived to regret the day I agreed to do it." She downed a hefty swallow of wine.

He shifted around to face her fully. His expression told her he'd come to a conclusion that tickled him.

"Never figured you for a coward, Jess."

"Coward?"

"You haven't seen it yet, have you?"

She thought about denying the truth, if for no other reason than to wipe that smirk off his handsome face. But he was right. She was a coward.

"No. I haven't seen it," she admitted. She didn't want to see it either. Seeing the proofs and knowing that one particular color photo of them had been blown up to marquee size for all of San Diego to see, had been quite enough.

She'd heard about it, though. She still logged her share of nine-to-five days writing copy and producing commercials for the station. While she'd tried to hole up in her office, she hadn't been able to avoid the necessary trips to the copier, the fax, or to Brian, the promotion manager. All week long she'd been the target of speculative looks, long wolf whistles, and campy innuendos poking good-natured fun.

"The phone has been ringing off the wall," Tony said.

"Requests to take it down?" she asked, tongue-in-cheek hopeful.

He chuckled. "Requests to turn up the heat. We're a hit, Foxie. The general consensus is that they want more."

"More? How could there possibly be more?" She thought of the provocative pose . . . and of the caption she herself had written:

THEN IT WAS RHETT AND SCARLETT
NOW IT'S TONY AND JESS

CLASSIC, ROMANTIC, SULTRY MUSIC UNTIL MIDNIGHT
TUNE IN TO THE FALCON AND THE FOX
AND LET THEM TAKE YOU INTO THE NIGHT
KXAL, 96.5 FM

She got light-headed just thinking about it. "What more could they possibly want?"

"More anything." His pause was ominous. "You'd just as well know it now. I gave Brian the go-ahead to start working on another shoot."

She groaned.

He grinned.

"So tell me, Jess. How do you feel about 'Me Tarzan, you Jane'?"

THREE

It took Jessie a minute to get her mouth to move; it took another to get her brain to coordinate. "You're not serious."

She could see by the look on his face that he was.

"Sorry, Jess, but you know as well as I do that sex sells. The station needs all the revenue we can generate. And I don't have to tell you, we've picked up some major accounts that want commercial time slots during our show."

No, he didn't have to tell her. She'd been writing the radio copy for some of those new accounts.

"Besides, if the listening audience wants romance," he went on, "it's our job to give it to them."

"And we do," she insisted, hoping her voice didn't reveal the panic she felt. "Monday, Wednesday, and Friday, seven P.M. until midnight. We give them great music, a request line, and a little titillating banter to take their minds off the rigors of their lives. But, Tony—"

"I know," he interrupted softly. "When you agreed to do the show, you hadn't bargained on it mushrooming the way it has."

"You've got that right. I hadn't bargained on a lot of things." Like that strange call that had come in on the request line the other night, she thought, shuddering.

". . . *you're making a mistake.* . . . *Stay away from him* . . ."

The voice, the words, had confused and shaken her then. The memory of the call shook her now. She buried it again, though, until she had time to review it rationally.

"And further," she continued, determined to make her limits clear to Tony, "I don't plan on exposing . . ." Her voice trailed off as she thought of all the body parts she'd have to expose in a Tarzan-Jane scenario. ". . . my poor judgment, just to satisfy a faceless audience's abstract sexual fantasies. Scarlett and Rhett was one thing. That was subtle. Suggestive, yes, but it was also sophisticated. Classic."

"Tarzan and Jane aren't classic?" Mischief danced in his dark eyes.

"Tarzan and Jane aren't clothed! At least not the way I remember them. Stop laughing at me."

"I'm sorry." He didn't sound sorry and he didn't stop laughing. "I told Brian you wouldn't go for it. I just didn't realize how much of a tiger you can be when you're mad. You can really show those claws, can't you?"

"Claws, yes. Tush, no. I mean it, Tony. No Tarzan. No Jane. No dice."

It wasn't just the exposure she was objecting to. It was the prospect of another day in Tony's arms posing for the camera. She'd barely survived *Gone With the Wind*. She wasn't about to be swept away on a swinging vine, not with him. Tony in nothing but a loincloth, baby oil, and a master-of-the-jungle grin would just about do her in.

"But you might consider something else?" he asked hopefully.

She released a heavy sigh, feeling her position slipping. "Is it really necessary?"

"Brian thinks so, yes. Judging by the response to the first billboard, he thinks a whole series of classic couples could be the most effective advertising blitz we've ever staged."

She thought of Brian Davis, baby-faced, balding, and in his mid-thirties. At least that was her best guess at his age, since she knew Brian and Tony had gone to college together. Looking at Brian, she never would have guessed he had the savvy or the spunk to deal with the demands of the promotion director's position. She'd changed her mind upon her first meeting with him, though. He was sharp, intelligent, and as aggressive when it came to business as he was shy when it came to personal contacts. As much as she liked him and found his quiet, reserved manner refreshing, she couldn't say she much cared for his stand on this billboard campaign.

"And what do you think?" she asked Tony, figuring she already knew the answer.

He shrugged. "I trust Brian's judgment. He's been with me since I took over the station, and he hasn't let me down yet. And let's face it. We didn't plan 'The Falcon and the Fox.' It was an accidental hit. But big-time revenues are often the result of accidents, and hits last only as long as the audience wants to be exposed to them. We need to help that exposure along. If the billboards are the vehicle to do it, then I think we'd better keep 'em coming. As a matter of fact Brian thinks he'll have something put together soon—*not* Tarzan and Jane," he assured her quickly when she started to speak.

Thoughtful, she stared into the fire. A warm hand on her bare foot stole her breath and set her heart thundering.

"It's just a few more photo shoots, Jess," he said softly. "And, I promise, you're going to love the billboard when you see it. You're right. It is a classic. You look . . ." His voice dropped to a low, husky pitch as his hand tightened on her foot. "You look absolutely incredible. I can see why we've gotten such positive responses."

Talk about positive responses, Jessie thought. She wished he'd take his hand off her foot, because she needed to breathe. Soon. It didn't appear that was going to happen if he continued to touch her. His hand was warm and large. His fingers were calloused and strong, yet his hold was achingly gentle.

She closed her eyes and prayed for strength.

She got a cat instead.

A huge Siamese sprang from nowhere and landed on her lap with a thud and a yowl, scaring a scream out of her and a hiss from the cat. There was one plus, however. The threat of death by oxygen deprivation had been eliminated. Heart attack suddenly seemed the most likely prospect.

"Tut!" Tony scolded the cat. Gathering the mass of inquisitive fur in his hands, he lifted the cat off Jessie's lap.

"Sorry about that." He set Tut aside and turned back to Jessie. "I should have warned you. He likes to surprise strangers. It's the one thing about the finicky critter I can count on. I just never know when he's going to stage it. Hey . . . you okay?"

Her face had gone ashen, her eyes round and unfocused. She smiled weakly. "Fine. I'm fine. I—I always scream like that when cats go for my face. I'm funny that way."

She was also very cute, whether she appreciated the adjective or not, Tony decided. He grinned at her stricken expression, until he realized he was the only one finding humor in the situation.

Oh, she was trying to be brave. But the fact of the matter was, he suspected she'd reached an emotional limit of sorts, and Tut's out-of-nowhere approach at hello had shoved her over the edge.

When he added up the events in her life of late,

he realized why she looked like she was about to crumble from the inside out. She was recently divorced, recently uprooted from the only home she'd ever known. New job, new responsibilities, financial commitments that were probably hard to meet, given all those changes plus tuition costs for her daughter. And while she hadn't talked about it, he knew the crank call they'd received the other night had shaken her.

That didn't even count tonight. She'd been stalled in the rain, drenched to her skin, then thought she was being stalked by a maniac cruising the freeway in a vehicle that defied description.

She'd been soaked and chilled and humiliated. And then Tut had added insult to injury by scaring her half out of her mind. While her situation didn't equate to a life-or-death struggle, it was enough.

"Jessie," he whispered as he eased up beside her on the sofa.

Smoky-gray eyes—eyes he hadn't realized until that moment were so seeking and needy—met his in a wide-eyed attempt at perky. The attempt failed miserably. One single tear spilled like a fat, salty raindrop onto her cheek.

She looked lost. And soft. And pretty.

"Ah, Jess," he murmured, settling a comforting arm over shoulders that felt as fragile as the rest of her looked. "If anybody ever needed a hug, I think it's you."

To his surprise she didn't fight him. She stiffened a little, but only at first. And only as a token resistance before she let him fold her into his arms and shelter her against his heart.

Against his heart. A heart that had suddenly come to life and was beating out the terms of the way she made him feel.

And just how the hell do *you feel, Falcone?* he asked himself as she snuggled against him. Protective? Damn straight he felt protective. Possessive? Like a king guarding his queen.

Without his sanctioning it, what had started as friendly comfort had changed in the space of a deep breath to something a far cry from fraternal.

Her hair caught on the stubble of his jaw as he tucked her head under his chin. He smoothed it back from her face and held her closer. The trembling that shuddered through her body, the feel of her hand resting against his chest, made him aware of his size. He was a big man; she was a small woman. Yet as he ran his hands in a soothing caress up and down her back, he suspected that he'd fit inside her just fine.

Warning bells clanged like a five-alarm fire. This line of thought had to stop. Now. But lower in his body a flame had already reached flash point and was quickly spreading out of control.

That was when his good intentions got shot all to hell.

He intended to set her away. Really he did. When he lowered his head to hers, it was with the hope that his brain would overrule his libido and spout out some catchy throwaway line that would help untangle them from each other's arms and set them back on the straight and narrow path. But she chose that same moment to tip her head back to look at him, to conjure, he was sure, the same kind of innocuous wordplay that would safely separate them.

His words didn't come. Neither did hers. She looked so hesitant, and so wounded, and so unsure, that he had no choice but to make that uncertainty go away. In that moment, with her eyes appealing to his to deny what they both should be fighting, it would have taken the Jaws of Life to pry his arms from around her.

If he had thought about it, he probably could have stopped it. But he wasn't capable of thinking. And that suited his purpose just fine. It didn't take any thought to cup her jaw in the hollow of his palm. No thought at all to trace the delicate rise of her cheekbone with his fingers, to brush the hair back from her temple and watch her eyes go liquid with an answering need.

Instinct, not logic, compelled him to lower his mouth to hers. Desire, not deduction, bid him catch her breath in his mouth when her soft sigh feathered across his lips. And sensation, not sense, insisted he tease her mouth open, then tempt her with his tongue to explore the newness of taste and texture, the wonders of honest response and melting arousal.

She tasted of rich red wine and honeyed longing. And just that fast he was lost. In her sweet, sultry heat. In the fine-boned body he dragged against his chest and fit against his hips. In the smoky eyes and the lacy web of lashes that fluttered, then dropped to cover them.

She was softer than a sigh, her response to his kiss more expressive than a poet writing about love. And she awoke in him a need as elemental as breathing, a desire as demanding as the thrumming of his pulse.

He pulled away only far enough to look into her eyes, only long enough to make sure what was happening was real. Then he lowered his head and lost himself in her again.

Jessie sank into his kiss, giving herself over to his tenderness, healing herself in his strength. She knew this shouldn't be happening. She knew that if she let it go on, it could lead to one of the biggest mistakes of her life.

His mouth on hers didn't feel like a mistake, though. It felt wonderful and right, a stunning contrast of soft invasion and steely demand . . . and it was a self-indulgence she couldn't deny.

Infinitely gentle yet boldly possessive, his arms made a welcome haven, the thundering of his heartbeat against her breast a triumphant healing. Her own heart soared at the strength of his reaction and the honesty of his physical response.

To think she could still do this to a man.

To think that a man like Tony wanted her because she was a desirable woman.

They were thoughts she couldn't let go of, just as his kiss was something she couldn't resist. Along with a fierce and fiery passion he kindled a resurgence of the self-esteem David had crushed a year ago when he'd left her.

David hadn't thrown away just their marriage. He'd thrown her away too. Like yesterday's news. Like an object that no longer held any value.

Tony's aggressive yet tender assault on her senses invited her to believe that as a woman, feminine, sensual, and strong, she was valuable after all.

She wanted to believe. And to experience. To feel the wonder of knowing that at this moment she was what he wanted. That *she* was responsible for the accelerated beat of his heart.

His kiss courted that belief and filled her with reckless satisfaction. She surrendered to his hunger, and with that surrender she came the closest to being in control that she'd felt in a long time.

It was wrong to let it go on. Intellectually she knew that. She also knew that playing by the rules hadn't garnered her the promised results. She'd been the devoted wife, she'd given willingly. Yet David had left her in spite of it all, and when he had, he'd taken with him everything that had made her a woman.

Tony wasn't taking, he was giving. The caress of his mouth on hers didn't feel anything but right. It felt as vital and alive as the silver falcon that pulsed with heat beneath her fingertips as she rested them against his throat.

It didn't matter that this had started out as a comforting embrace. What mattered was the healing promise of pleasure following months of self-doubt and pain. What mattered was that Tony had been as taken by surprise as she had when comfort had turned into something else.

Something more substantial, more seductive, and more demanding than even she had bargained for.

Kindness had given way to intrigue, and intrigue to spontaneous combustion and a fire that had struck like summer lightning.

She felt the electric energy of the storm in his arms and couldn't resist riding with the thunder. She closed her eyes and enjoyed the thrill of her heartbeat answering his; the feel of his jaw, stubbled and strong; the groan that reverberated from his chest to his throat, erotic and arousing, a testimony to the desire he felt for her.

Just a little longer, she promised as she sank into his heat, opening her mouth wide to accept the deeper stroke of his tongue, nestling her hip into the hard evidence of his arousal.

Just a little longer, she pleaded. Just a little more of this conflicting and heady sense of vulnerability and control. Another taste of his tongue, another delicious whisper of his mouth across her jaw and skating down her neck, the fire of his breath burning both savage and sweet.

She trembled with wonder and with wanting as he nudged the robe aside. The velvet stroke of his tongue coupled with the gentle nip of his teeth sent a delicious shimmer of need pulsing through her . . . along with a swift and sobering awareness of how far her self-indulgence had gone.

Tony felt the change in her. She didn't have to say

anything. She didn't have to push him away. He felt the transition as passion turned to panic and she began pulling back emotionally.

He stilled, then tensed, then swore with the effort to get himself under control. He felt a deep breath shudder through her, and he wasn't sure if her tremulous sigh was prompted by relief or regret.

Forced by necessity but undercut by desire, he came back to his senses slowly. It was no mean feat. He'd liked being lost in her just fine. From the way she'd been responding, he'd have sworn she'd been in no hurry to be found either. Yet she'd put on the skids, and he was left trying to figure out why.

When he thought he could finally risk it, he curled a finger under her chin and forced her to meet his gaze. Her beautiful eyes were still glazed with passion, but he saw flashes of panic and denial.

He didn't want her panicked. He didn't want her sorry.

He just wanted her.

As he watched the emotions play across her face, felt the heat of her breath fan his jaw, and felt the trembling of her body, he knew he could still have her. She was that vulnerable, that close to being out of control.

It wouldn't take much to tumble her over the edge with him. Another kiss. A whispered word. An intimate caress of his mouth to the sweetness of her bare flesh, and she'd melt, as he was melting at the thought of finishing what he'd never intended to start. He knew all the right moves, had employed them more often than he cared to remember.

He was tempted. Lord, he was tempted to risk it all for the pleasure her hot and wild response promised. But as much as he wished it were otherwise, her eyes told him that tonight was not the night to ask her to make good on that promise.

Although he suspected she'd fervently deny it, she was as fragile as hand-blown glass right then. Her trembling wasn't all passion. It was tension and disbelief, and it reflected the tenuous grasp she had on her dignity. If he sullied that dignity, he'd never be able to look himself in the mirror again. That hadn't always been a consideration for him. With Jessie, however, it was suddenly his utmost concern.

So much for his good intentions, he thought with chagrin. This had all started because he'd felt a need to comfort her. Yet in one *brilliant* testosterone-fueled move, he had added to her turmoil instead of decreasing it.

"It's all right, Jess," he whispered, determined to set things right. He cupped her head between his palms. "Come on, Jess, it really is okay."

Her eyes told him she was far from convinced.

He hated this, hated feeling like a heel. He'd always enjoyed open relationships with women. Romance without commitment. Knowledge of those ground rules was a prerequisite. It eliminated hassles in the long run. And the long run did not involve complex emotional entanglements. He was a simple man. He worked hard, he played hard. He loved his boisterous Italian family, his work, his independence, and his cat, in that order. And he did not become involved with women who didn't understand that up front.

Yet here he was, balancing on the brink of involvement with a woman who made him want to forget all those rules.

"Come on, Jess. It was only a kiss," he said, checking the urge to draw her into his arms again.

When she lowered her eyes, he tipped her chin up and forced her to look at him. "Only a kiss," he repeated. "Only a nice, friendly kiss. Okay," he conceded, grinning when she reddened. "So it was *more* than friendly. So it was *better* than nice. It was terrific. But it was still only a kiss. It didn't go any farther. It doesn't ever have to."

Like hell it didn't, he thought as he watched her face. While he didn't exactly know where this was going, he knew it was far from over. Far from begun, even. He knew it. She knew it. And while he wasn't going to make her face that truth tonight, neither was he going to let the implication fade too far into the background.

"Evidently it was a curiosity we both felt a need to satisfy, or it wouldn't have happened, right?"

The look in her eyes was all the acknowledgment he needed.

"And I'm not sorry about it, Jess. Let me off the hook here and tell me you're not sorry either."

She pinched her eyes shut, tipped her head back, and swallowed hard.

"Hey . . ." He touched his thumb to her throat, drew it in a gentle stroke to the hollow where tense muscle worked against the sculptured protrusion of her collarbone. "Don't. Please don't be embarrassed. I'm a big boy. I wouldn't have let you hurt me."

That absurdity finally brought a laugh. It was colored with a hint of desperation, but it was a laugh, and he was glad to hear it. Glad to see her relaxing, if only by a degree.

"I'm a physical man, Jess. I'm a toucher. I act on what feels right. It felt right. And it was." He shook her slightly, playfully. "Besides, what do you expect? I'm Italian."

Another smile. This one on the heels of an exaggerated roll of her eyes.

"I liked kissing you," he went on matter-of-factly, letting her get used to the idea. "I'm glad you liked kissing me. So as far as I can see, since we both liked it, we have no problem. And no regrets—for either of us, okay?

"And you've got to admit," he added, not wanting to minimize what had happened, "considering it was only a kiss, it was a hell of a ride."

"A hell of a ride," she echoed softly. "Seems to be the theme for my night tonight. One wild ride after another."

He worked hard on a scowl. "So much for compliments. You've reduced my kiss to the equivalent of your fiasco on the freeway and the ride in my nephew's van. But I'm not going to take offense. Lucky for you I've got a strong ego."

At last a genuine smile. She met his eyes levelly, her composure finally gaining more than a toehold. "And lucky for me you are a very nice man."

"Yeah, well, don't let it get around. Everyone at the station thinks I'm an ogre. Works for me, though. Keeps 'em all in line."

Her expression darkened at the mention of the station.

"This changes nothing at work, Jess," he said, sensing the direction her thoughts had taken. "I don't want you worrying about that. I'm still your boss. You're still one of the crew. No new extracurricular expectations attached to the job because of this, okay?"

She looked at him carefully, as if weighing the truth of his statement. It stung that she would doubt him, but he suspected her self-preservation mechanism was running in high gear right about now. So when she finally nodded and murmured a quiet "okay," he forgave her for it.

He figured he'd forgive her just about anything. There was something about her, perhaps that vulnerability she'd been revealing all evening. He knew it came not from weakness but from a wound that he suspected had cut deep and had not yet fully healed. Balancing that vulnerability was a strength that made her persevere in the face of that obstacle.

He'd known a lot of women and he'd loved his share of them. But he'd never experienced this spontaneous sense of propriety before. It set him on edge to realize that besides burning to make love to her, he wanted to be the one to heal her hurts too. He wanted to be the one to dispel the pain.

The implications were monumental, the major one being commitment. There it was again—commitment—a concept he'd never before entertained. It was something he was going to have to think about. A lot.

To do that, he would have to get her out of his house before he chucked this "no big deal, it's only a kiss and it changes nothing between us" bull and picked up where they'd just left off.

"So . . ." He dipped his head to hers, gave her shoulders a fraternal squeeze, and forced a quick smile. "Why don't you go check to see if your clothes are dry, then I'll give you a lift home."

"You don't need to do that."

He touched her hair again, then pulled away when he realized what a hard time he was having not touching her. "Yes, I do. I think it's pretty obvious that you can't stay here."

A telling look flashed from her eyes to his. He groaned and rose from the sofa while he still had the strength of character to talk himself out of talking her into staying the night.

"I meant you didn't have to drive me. I can call a cab," she said softly.

"No. You can't. The fare would break you, and I'd feel like a heel turning you over to a complete stranger. Now, go on. Go check on those clothes."

It took his last ounce of restraint to keep from following her into his bedroom, knowing that when she got there, she was going to slip his robe from her shoulders and stand naked by his bed before she put her clothes back on.

With a muffled curse he headed for the kitchen. He snagged the keys from the peg by the back door and waited with his hand anchored to the doorknob until she joined him.

The ride to her apartment was long and tense.

So was the night alone in his bed.

FOUR

Sarah's visit the next day was the bright spot of Jessie's Sunday. Or at least it would have been if her daughter hadn't been so perceptive.

"It's not a good idea to hold things in, you know," Sarah said, her doe-brown eyes meeting Jessie's over a Yankee pot roast, glazed carrots, mashed potatoes, and a fruit salad. "It's much better to talk things out."

Jessie set down her fork and put on her best imitation of a puzzled smile. "Honey, I don't know what you're talking about. Everything's fine."

"The last time I saw circles like that under your eyes, you said everything was fine too."

The look Sarah gave her squeezed Jessie's heart and brought the sting of tears to her eyes. Sometimes her little girl was far too wise. Today she was much too worried.

Guilt grabbed Jessie by the throat and wouldn't

let go. A pretty twenty-year-old's biggest concern should be acing a test on the history of modern civilization or deciding which guy's heart she was going to break that week. She shouldn't be worrying about whether her mother was going to fall apart the way Jessie had before coming to grips with David's departure.

Sarah had suffered, too, during and since the divorce. She missed her father. She missed the sense of family. And Jessie would never forgive herself for letting it be Sarah who had found her that day broken and out of control.

She reached across the table and covered Sarah's hand with her own. "I'm okay, sweetie," she assured her, needing to dispel the shadows of worry that hovered on her daughter's face. "I just didn't get much sleep last night is all. After I left you, my stupid car stalled on the freeway. It made for a long and miserable night."

It wasn't a lie; it was just a half-truth. She couldn't see herself telling her daughter that the real reason she hadn't slept much the night before was because Tony Falcone had kissed her into meltdown and left her as charged as a nuclear reactor.

Praying her cheeks didn't give away the residual heat she felt just thinking about him, she concentrated on shoving her food around her plate with her fork.

Her explanation marginally mollified her daughter. "You're going to have to break down and get a new car, Mom. That thing's been a lemon ever since you bought it."

Jessie rose to get more milk from the refrigerator. "Not in the cards." She refilled Sarah's glass. "Not yet anyway. My budget is stressed to the max as it is."

As soon as she said it, she could have bitten her tongue. She was real Mother of the Year material that evening. Sarah needed to worry about finances like Jessie needed another stretch mark.

She made it a point not to minimize David's image to Sarah. Sarah loved her father. Jessie didn't want that to change, and it surely would if Sarah knew how stingy David had been in the divorce settlement. New loves required money for flowers and jewelry, Jessie thought, finding a twisted humor where once she'd felt only pain.

"The budget is stretched by my choice, Sarah. Other things take priority at the moment—like a real snappy outfit I've got my eye on at a little boutique down in Old Town," she lied. "Now, I don't want you worrying about money. I'm getting by just fine. How's your dinner?" she asked, hedging away from the subject.

"Great. I can't tell you how much I look forward to these home-cooked meals. Cafeteria food is all starch and sugar. It's like they want to keep us wired so we can stay awake in class. Speaking of classes . . ." She paused and met her mother's eyes across the table. "I wish you'd let me get a job. I don't need to go to school this summer."

Jessie shook her head. "You do if you want to

finish on schedule. Honey, I want you to get your education, and I want you to get it behind you as soon as possible—"

"But I could help with expenses."

"Not necessary," she said, though her heart swelled with pride over Sarah's adult sense of responsibility. "Money is not an issue."

"Then why can't you get a new car?"

"I like that car," Jessie insisted, hoping she wouldn't choke on the words. "It's the carburetor I could do without." She smiled, then added firmly, "No job. Subject closed. Eat your dinner."

Something about warm water and soapsuds loosened the tongue. Maybe it was the memories associated with hundreds of similar after-dinner scenes of mother and daughter sharing kitchen duty. Maybe it was the contentment of a full tummy and a good meal. In any event it was while they were washing the dishes that Sarah broached the subject of David.

"I spoke with Dad last night after you dropped off the laptop."

With staged concentration Jessie scrubbed a saucepan, schooling any show of emotion from her face. "He called you?"

"Um-hmm. Just checking to see how things are going."

"Well, I'm sure he worries about you," she said generously.

"He worries about you too," Sarah said in a leading tone.

Jessie was beyond bitterness and would have masked it even if she hadn't been. "Old habits are hard to break, I guess."

Uncharacteristically quiet, Sarah wiped a dinner plate, then set it on a cupboard shelf. "He'd like to see you, Mom."

That was not news. Jessie had heard from David too. He'd included a note with the check for his share of Sarah's summer-quarter tuition expenses. She'd chalked it up to a necessary meeting concerning Sarah. The anticipation in Sarah's voice, however, suggested otherwise and brought Jessie's head around.

"He misses you."

There it was again, Jessie thought. Hope. It was threaded through every one of Sarah's words. She physically felt Sarah's excitement. Once, so very long ago, she would have shared it.

She dried her hands and looked up at her daughter, who had inherited her father's height and stood several inches taller than Jessie. "Honey," she said, carefully choosing her words, "your father made his choice when he filed for divorce. I had to learn to live with it. Now he has to live with it too."

"He made a mistake, Mom. He realizes it now."

Jessie closed her eyes and let her chin drop to her chest. *Damn you, David*, she swore silently, as maternal anger begged to break free. Damn you for ripping our family apart and now using our daughter to undo the damage.

"Well," she began, tamping down on that anger, willing her voice to sound objective, "I'm sure he'll manage to work through it. We did. We have. We are," she added for emphasis, and gave Sarah a bright smile. "When you talk to him again, tell him hello for me and that I hope things are going well for him. By the way, have you decided yet if you're going back to KC to spend the Memorial Day holiday weekend with him?"

"I guess." She sounded glum. "I wish you were coming too. Wouldn't it be great to see Gram and Grampa again?"

Jessie hadn't seen her parents or her sister and her family since she'd relocated to San Diego.

"Of course I'd love to see them, but a trip home is going to have to wait for a while. Maybe this fall."

"If it's money, Dad hinted that he'd pay your airfare."

Regardless of the hope still hovering in Sarah's eyes, Jessie knew this conversation about David needed closure. She was about to give it that, when her doorbell rang and took care of it for her.

Sarah's gaze shot from the door to her mother. "Expecting someone?"

Jessie shook her head, dried her hands, and skirted the central island that separated her small kitchen from the living area.

She looked through the security peephole and froze. Tony stood on the other side.

"Who is it?" Sarah asked from behind her.

How exactly should she answer that? My boss? My cohost? My designated heartbeat accelerator? Good Lord, a woman her age should *not* be experiencing these sorts of heavy-duty palpitations. She could sprain something.

Pasting on a plucky smile, she latched a hand onto the knob and swung the door open.

"Tony. Hi," she said brightly, and turned back to Sarah. "You remember Mr. Falcone, don't you, Sarah?"

Sarah straightened immediately, running her hand through her long blond hair in a quick, unconscious, and totally feminine gesture of awareness sparked by the presence of a good-looking man. "Sure. Hello, Mr. Falcone."

"Hey, Sarah." Tony smiled that knee-melting smile, then turned his deep, dark eyes to Jessie. "And hello to you. How are you today?"

It was more than a casual hello. It was less than an intimate caress. But not much.

"Fine. Fine," she squeaked, and escaped the real questions in his eyes in favor of the questions in Sarah's.

"Would you believe it? Tony's the one who found me trudging along in the rain last night after my car gave up. He brought me home."

"Oh." Sarah's measuring gaze flitted from her mother to Tony.

"And that's what brings me back today," he said easily. He fished in the pocket of his snug, well-worn jeans and tugged out Jessie's car keys. "I brought your car back. It's parked down in your space."

"It's running?"

"Yup. Remember Stan with the tow truck? He's also a weekend mechanic. I went over there this morning and we got her going again. It wasn't the carburetor," he added in response to her puzzled frown. "Loose wire. Anyway she's running fine for the moment."

"Well . . ." Jessie realized she still had a death grip on the doorknob. Prying her fingers away, she tucked her hands into the back pockets of her jeans. "It would seem I owe you again."

"Purely self-serving motives. I don't want you to be late for work tomorrow."

She'd fought it as long as she could—that undeniable tug on her heart, that need to be enveloped by his warmth. She softened and returned his smile. "Shades of Simon Legree. I knew you weren't the marshmallow everyone said you were."

"Yeah, well, that goes to show you can't always believe what you hear." He flashed her another one of those sexy-as-sin grins, then winked at Sarah. "Got to go. Just wanted to deliver the goods and make sure you survived the night."

Survived was an uncannily accurate choice of words.

"At least let me give you a ride home," she said.

"Or I could take you," Sarah chimed in, working hard at affecting an "I'm much older than I look"

look that did not slip by her mother unnoticed. "I was just about to leave anyway."

"While it's hard to pass up not one but two tempting offers, Stan's waiting to do the deed. He followed me in his truck to make sure our mechanical skills are as good as we like to think they are."

"Well, then . . ." Jessie hesitated, not wanting him to go, knowing he absolutely, positively, unquestionably could not stay. "Until you're better paid, I thank you."

"Until I'm better paid," he repeated in a slow, purposeful drawl that suggested a world of possible paybacks he'd like to explore. None of them monetary. All of them seductive. "See you tomorrow, Jess."

She could only nod.

"Sarah, it was nice seeing you again." With that he was out the door, closing it soundly behind him.

Unable to move, Jessie stared at that closed door and groped for her lost bearings.

Behind her, Sarah sighed dreamily. "What a man."

"A very nice man," Jessie agreed as her thoughts echoed and added to her daughter's sentiments. Nice. Gorgeous. Temptingly sexy in tailored suits or, as he was dressed today, in worn and faded denim and a grease-streaked T-shirt.

"Too bad he's too old for me." Sarah smiled wistfully, then added with just a hint of playful warning, "Too bad *you're* too old for him."

Bull's-eye. That one pierced dead center and sank

deep. Jessie looked down to see if she was bleeding on the carpet.

"Otherwise," Sarah continued speculatively, "I'd begin to wonder along with my friends if you two really do have something going on."

Jessie paled. Loss of blood, probably. "I beg your pardon?"

"The request line, Mom. Everybody listens. You guys are great. If I didn't know it was my mom who was the Fox playing to the Falcon, I'd swear you two had the hots for each other."

Jessie caught a glimmer of doubt in Sarah's eyes, the wonder, the need for confirmation that their on-air relationship was just part of the hype for "The Falcon and the Fox" show.

"Acting!" she stated with dramatic flare, mimicking a popular comedian whose routine parodied an aging thespian taken with his own acting abilities.

They both laughed.

Jessie stopped abruptly, though, when she realized she hadn't yet prepared Sarah for another offshoot of the show.

"Our show has become pretty popular. That's good for business."

"That's great, Mom."

"Business needs to be cultivated to keep it growing."

"And that's why you play up the romance angle, right?"

Jessie nodded, took a deep breath, and decided to go for it.

Sarah stopped her. "I've seen the billboard, Mom."

"Oh." Her breath deflated from her lungs. "I was hoping I'd get to you first. But I hadn't worked up the nerve to tell you." She met her daughter's eyes with great reluctance. "So, what do you think?"

"Truth?"

Jessie sank down on the sofa and nodded as she stared at her clasped hands.

"I think . . . it's great!"

Her head shot up. "Really?"

"Really."

"You don't think it's too much?" She watched Sarah's face closely for signs of discomfort.

Sarah sat beside her and took both of Jessie's hands in hers. "You look absolutely beautiful. It makes me very proud. And a little jealous. You want to know what the guys say?" Sarah's eyes sparkled with mischief.

"Oh, gee, Sarah, I think I'd really like to skip that."

"They say the Fox is the real thing. A real fox. And they want to know if my mom is as hot as she looks."

Jessie groaned.

Sarah laughed and jumped up from the sofa. "Got to run. I'm meeting Kyle for a study date."

"Kyle? *The* Kyle?" Jessie baited. Sarah, it seemed, was doing better with the billboard than she herself was. "The one who's the best thing since chocolate, ice cream, and bubble bath all rolled into one?"

"That would be him."

"When did this happen?" she asked, following Sarah to the door.

"Just did. And I owe it to you."

"Me?"

"Someone told him Jessie Fox's daughter was on campus, and he came looking for me. Said he figured you'd have a fox for a daughter too."

"You're kidding, right?"

Sarah grinned noncommittally.

Jessie decided to take that as affirmative, because it was too ludicrous to deal with if she was serious. "And is he as nice as you say he is gorgeous?"

"Time will tell, but it's starting out that way."

"Just go carefully, honey, okay?"

"You worry too much." With that Sarah kissed Jessie good-bye, jokingly but pointedly reminded her that it was a good thing she was too old for the Falcon, and bounced out the door.

Too old, Jessie echoed silently, closing the door behind her daughter. Too foolish even to think about him.

Tucking her hands in the hip pockets of her jeans, she turned to face her empty apartment.

Too lonely.

She didn't want to, but Jessie made herself do it. On her way to the station Monday afternoon, she detoured via Mission Gorge Road. It was time to face the billboard.

On the first drive by, she went into shock.

On the second, she nearly rear-ended a Toyota.

It wasn't until her third pass that she had the presence of mind to pull off onto a frontage road and park in a fast-food parking lot that afforded an ogler's eye view.

For minutes after she shut off the ignition all she could do was stare.

It was all there, larger than life and in brilliant, living color, for everyone to see. Every nuance, every shivering sexual spark that had passed between them. And the effect was as beautiful as it was breathtaking.

Tony was magnificent. Staged against a backdrop depicting the antebellum South, he looked every glorious inch the romantic rascal, Rhett Butler, as Gable had portrayed him. His black hair was dramatically slicked back, his dark eyes sexually commanding as he dared her with a look that pitted dominance against desire.

Her gaze was drawn from his eyes and the sinfully thick lashes that the camera had captured so vividly, to the seductive curve of his mouth, the breadth of his shoulders covered in fawn-colored broadcloth, and finally to his hands.

She remembered the burn of those strong hands that appeared to hold her captive. She remembered the feel of those long, elegant fingers spread possessively around her ribs, dangerously close to the underswell of her breast.

In a daze she shifted her attention to Scarlett and

reconciled herself to the fact that it was actually she, Jessie Fox, meeting Tony's searing gaze.

Tony and Sarah were right. She *did* look incredible. With her hair pulled back into a snood ornamented with rhinestones and her face powdered to porcelain perfection, she was a worthy match for Tony's Rhett. In her eyes shone a vibrant fire; in her expression passion flared with an arresting combination of vulnerability and desire. The red satin dress left her shoulders bare, the dramatic V-neckline barely concealed her breasts and the dusky shadow of cleavage.

The looks passing between them sizzled with sexual awareness. The excitement was palpable, the enticement subtle, yet erotic.

Classic drama. Breathless anticipation.

"A reenactment," she reminded herself sternly.

A reality, the voice of truth countered.

She sighed deeply. *A reason to get a grip.*

This could not continue. Tightening her hands on the steering wheel, she dropped her head against the seat back and wondered if she could possibly sell Tony on the idea of Raggedy Ann and Andy as the next classic couple. Or maybe Edith and Archie Bunker. Al and Peg Bundy. Fred and Wilma Flintstone . . .

"Until tomorrow, children, that's it for the Fat Man. I'll be calling it a wrap, but you all stay tuned now, you hear? Coming your way from now until that magic midnight hour is the hottest thing to hit the West Coast since last summer's heat wave. The Falcon and the Fox, San Diego's answer to the energy crisis, are up next with five hours of music, romance, and requests to heat up your night. Enjoy."

Jessie grinned at Dan "The Fat Man" Brannigan as he eased out from behind the radio board and she sat down in his place.

"Hey, Jessie, how's it going?"

Where the handle "The Fat Man" came from, Jessie had no idea. Dan Brannigan was a tall beanpole of a man with a wiry cap of bright red hair and a quick, irreverent sense of humor.

"Fine, Dan. How's Nancy?"

"Big as a barn and ornery as sin. If that baby doesn't pop soon, I swear the woman is going to blow a gasket. Other than that, she's doing great."

"Well, tell her to hang in there, okay?"

"You got it. Have a good show now." With that he breezed out the on-air studio door.

Jessie reached for her headphones and shot a glance toward the clock. Six fifty-eight and counting. Tony had less than two minutes to show time, and no one had seen him at the station all afternoon.

He's probably afraid you'll attack him between the theme song and the first number, she told herself in disgust. And who could blame him?

She pinched her eyes shut and drew a deep breath, trying to shake off the embarrassment that sent her heart into a tripping tango every time she thought about Saturday night. It didn't matter that she'd rationalized what had happened between them a hundred different ways during two long sleepless nights that had been fraught with recrimination and regret. She was still embarrassed. He probably was too—not for himself but for her.

Getting back to the business at hand, she organized the radio copy she'd produced in the production room during the past two hours and looked over her show prep, all the while trying to put things in perspective.

Sarah's visits always reminded Jessie that part of her problem was that even though she'd gotten over David, she still missed being married. Like Sarah she missed the family concept. Not that she felt she needed a man to complete her life. She'd just liked having someone to complement it. Someone to share with.

She'd enjoyed the partnership and missed the emotional intimacy as much as she missed the sex. To that end, though, she wasn't about to indulge in the latter just because she didn't see any promise of the former—even though, thanks to Tony, it was the physical part that was giving her the most trouble. Sex might temporarily relieve some specific anxieties, but it wouldn't resolve anything long-term.

Tony Falcone definitely wasn't long-term material. She avoided office gossip like the plague, but unless one worked in a vacuum, it was impossible not to pick up on scattered scraps of dialogue bandied about the station. By all accounts Tony was a man who preferred his women to be at least as pretty as he was, and he changed partners as often as he changed shirts. Not the kind of man to pin a future on.

If she ever entered into a relationship again, it would be with someone solid and dependable. Someone who would appreciate her maturity over her bust size. Someone she could grow old with, not grow up with. Someone her own age. Which this man definitely was not.

So why did you turn Steven down? she asked herself. He was everything she'd just told herself she wanted. Solid. Dependable. Mature. He just hadn't been enough.

What she needed, she thought glumly, was a combination of the two. Steven's steadiness and Tony's sex appeal. Lord, was she really that shallow? Or was it more than Tony's physical appeal that drew her to him?

"Well, you'll never know, Fox," she muttered under her breath. "Because *nothing* is ever going to happen between you and Mr. Falcone. Period. End of discussion."

She made another furtive glance at the clock just as the minute hand ticked to seven straight up and the final notes of Mariah Carey's latest hit echoed to a close.

Speaking of dependable, she thought, it was show time. "Where the devil are you, Tony?" she whispered to the empty room as she potted up their theme song, "Into the Night."

"And a good, good evening to you out there," she said, adjusting her levels on the board as she ramped over the dramatically seductive piano intro. "This is Jessie Fox, and I'll be with you from now until midnight with the sweetest sounds, the smoothest notes, and the Falcon himself to keep us company. Call us. We'll be waiting . . ."

"Don't make a liar out of me, Falcone," she muttered when she'd flicked off the mike.

She was pulling a few CDs to fill time until the first request came in, when the door opened behind her.

"Sorry I'm late," Tony whispered as he eased into the studio and took his seat across the radio board from her.

He looked breathless, ruffled, and positively dangerous as he ran his fingers through his hair to smooth it. Slipping on his headset, he flashed her a sheepish grin.

"Traffic?" she suggested, forcing a casualness she was far from feeling.

He snorted. "I should be so lucky. A new client got me cornered in her office and wouldn't let me out."

She tilted her head in doubt.

"I swear to God, Jess. The woman was a barracuda. I mean, I've dodged my share of come-ons— hell, we all have—but this woman was as determined as they come."

"Tied you up, did she?"

"Damn near." He shuddered as if contemplating the outcome if he hadn't gotten away.

She fought a grin. "So, did you get the account?"

His eyes danced in triumph. "Damn right."

In spite of her earlier tension she laughed. "Like the Texas rangers, you always get your woman, huh?"

"Always." He slanted her an intimate look. "How are you, by the way?"

How was she? Certifiable, she'd guess. One minute she was talking her way around her feelings for him, the next she was melting with anticipation.

"Fine. I'm fine." Unable to hold his gaze, she glanced at the CD player as the red digits rolled off the seconds. "Down to fifteen."

"Right. So, are we set here?"

"Ready to rock and roll."

"Let's do it."

The music ebbed to its end. Slipping in the next CD, Tony adjusted his levels on the board and flipped on his mike.

"Hello, San Diego. I see my lady warmed you up. I know the feeling. She does that to me too. And now I'm here with her, and together we're really going to turn up the heat."

On cue Jessie broke in as if they'd been working together for years. "We want to hear from you. This is your station for love. Music that's right for the night . . ."

"Straight from the heart . . ." Tony's slow, seductive rasp drifted through the room like a sultry promise. "We're always ready to take your requests . . ."

"And take you into the night. All your favorite songs . . ."

"Here on one station. Ninety-six and a half, FM. Call me if you want to win that special lady's heart."

"Or me, if he needs that little nudge in the right direction. We'll play your love song . . ."

"You figure out the rest. That's the fun part, right, Jess?"

She laughed, mellow and seductive. And an act, she told herself. "If you say so, Tony. And now here's Toto with one of my favorites from last year, 'Call It Love.' "

Tony eased in, talking over the musical intro. "If you say so, Jess."

The suggestion, though staged for the listening audience, shimmered in the air and in his eyes as he flipped off his mike and met her gaze across the board.

Spellbound, she couldn't look away.

When one of the two phone lines reserved for requests lit up, Tony reluctantly broke the eye contact. "Looks like we're off and running."

"Looks like," she replied in a choppy voice, and picked up on the other line when it, too, lit up.

As they'd come to expect, the next five hours kept them running, hunting, and a bit breathless, but Jessie was thankful that it gave her some emotional distance to think about how Tony made her feel. A bigger station would have had a main switchboard to screen calls, then relay them to the DJs. KXAL wasn't a bigger station. The calls came in on two lines direct and made for some fast thinking and sometimes some hairy moments.

"Thank God for my cassette," Jessie said, stepping around Tony and stretching to reach a Foreigner CD on the top shelf of the library. "I've got a live-one ready for after the next set. Says his girlfriend locked herself in the bathroom and figures a dedication will help bring her out."

Tony chuckled. Finding the recording he wanted, he swung back to his chair. He tucked the CD into place and slipped his headset back on just as the last song faded to a close.

"Here's something special just for you, Debbie. Butch says he's sorry. Cut the poor guy some slack, okay? If you won't do it for him, do it for me. And do it for yourself. You know you want to."

He raised the volume of the song, flipped off his mike, and turned back to her, picking up the conversation where they'd left off. "Locked in the bathroom, huh? Did you get it on tape?"

She nodded and slumped back in her chair, feeling both the exhaustion and the exhilaration of the busy night. "It's ready to pot up next."

They'd both learned early on that airing phone calls live was risky business. While a reel-to-reel ran twenty-four hours a day recording all the on-air programming, Jessie used a cassette to catch the request calls and hold for playback later. Tony preferred to use the delay button on his side of the board.

"Thank the powers that be that we can call this a wrap in"—she glanced at the clock—"fifteen minutes."

"Amen to that. It's been a wild one."

Her phone line lit up again, punctuating Tony's accurate summation.

"Ninety-six and a half, FM. This is Jessie. Thanks for calling 'Into the Night.' "

Dead silence. The same dead silence that had preceded the call last week and had set her on edge and expectant ever since.

She willed herself to be calm. Told herself she was being foolish and was simply primed to be spooked.

"This is Jessie," she repeated carefully. "Did you have a request?"

"You didn't listen."

Her heart hit her ribs like a hammer. It was him. The same man who had called last week. There was no mistaking his voice. Sinister with warning, ice cold with intent. She closed her eyes and swallowed back a lump of apprehension.

"Who . . . who is this?" she asked breathlessly as her gaze shot to Tony's.

She could see in his eyes that he'd picked up on her distress. He whipped off his headset, punched in on the line, and let the voice echo through the studio on the speaker phone.

"I had a request last week, Jessie," the caller continued in that same lethal, menacing cadence. "You ignored it. So let's try again. Stay away from him."

"S-stay away from who?"

"Falcone. Stay away from him, or he's going to get hurt."

The line went dead.

Jessie swallowed tightly and closed her eyes, willing her heart to steady and slow.

Across the four feet of radio board separating them, she heard Tony swear, softly, succinctly, above the ominous drone of the dial tone.

FIVE

Over an hour had passed since they'd turned the studio over to Jason Strong, a college student who earned extra cash baby-sitting the preprogrammed format for the midnight-to-five-thirty shift.

Tony watched Jessie carefully as they played back both that night's and the previous week's recordings that had captured their mystery caller's voice and messages.

She was still visibly shaken. Her face was as pale as her white silk blouse. Her eyes burned fever bright. Her small hands were gripped tightly together on the desk in the production room.

They'd already played the "let's minimize this situation" game, and both had come up losers. One call they could toss away as a prank. Two calls they had to take seriously.

"Well," Jessie said when the second tape had ended, "there's no mistaking. It's the same voice."

Her own voice was reedy, her expression resigned to the truth. It ate at Tony's gut to see her torment and know that for now at least he could do nothing about it. He felt helpless and angry and wished that what he was thinking weren't true. Someone was out there. Someone who meant business. Some way he had to figure out what kind of business this joker had in mind.

"You were right," he agreed finally, swiping a hand over his lower jaw. "It's the same guy. Dammit, Jess, I'm sorry."

Puzzled, she looked up at him. *"You're* sorry? You're not responsible for this."

"No, but I am responsible for you."

"I beg your pardon?"

He smiled grimly at the fire in her eyes that burned through the helplessness she must be feeling. Vulnerable and independent. An arresting combination. She was too much, this lady.

"As your employer," he clarified, "I'm responsible for your safety. I should have taken precautions."

"As if you could have done something to prevent this."

"Yeah," he said glumly, angry at his stupidity, damning hindsight as a poor substitution for foresight. "There's something I could have done. If I was going to put you on the air, I should have planned on the possibility of this happening. We never should have used your real name. A radio name would at least have protected your identity."

She rubbed her arms as if trying to ward off a

chill. "Well, who knew something like this would happen when we started the show."

It was a statement, not a question, and it was totally devoid of accusation. It shouldn't have been, Tony thought. She should be mad as hell at him.

He ran a punishing hand through his hair. "*I* should have known, Jess. *I* should have been prepared. The world is full of crazies. More than a fair share of them call southern California home."

If he'd had any inkling that she was going to do more than fill in that one night, he'd have insisted on a radio name for her then and there. For that matter he'd have come up with one for himself too. The "fanatic fan" who developed fixations on DJs was unfortunately more commonplace than the general public suspected. It was a serious problem, and he should have seen it coming.

"Tony," she asked after a long, uncomfortable silence, "do you really think this guy is a problem?"

He cupped his hand behind his neck and slumped back in his chair. "I don't know. I think he'd like to make us believe he is. And I think he wants to scare you. Yet it's funny. He's calling you, but the threats are directed toward me."

She considered that. "Play the tapes one more time, would you? I want to listen again."

He wound back the tape of the previous week's call and punched the play button.

"*Ninety-six and a half, FM. This is Jessie. Thanks for calling 'Into the Night.'*"

Silence, then Jessie's voice again.

"Hello. This is Jessie. If you're there, I can't hear you. Did you have a request?"

"You're making a mistake."

Again silence filled the room as they listened, then Jessie's hesitant *"I'm sorry. I didn't catch that."*

"Yes you did. Stay away from him."

A click, then a dial tone as the connection was broken.

"Anything this time?" Tony asked as he stopped the tape and met her eyes.

She shook her head, her delicate brows furrowed. "No. Nothing. I keep thinking I'll hear something in the voice that I'll recognize. Sometimes I almost grasp a thread, but then just as quickly it's gone. I can't make a connection with anything—or anyone. And I can't say that I hear a threat either. It's more like an order. Let's hear the other one."

Tony ejected the cassette, traded it for that night's, and after a quick rewind punched the play button.

"Ninety-six and a half, FM. This is Jessie. Thanks for calling 'Into the Night.'"

Together they listened again to that eerie, ominous silence. Together they waited for Jessie's voice to come back on the line. Neither of them missed the tentative edge in her tone.

"This is Jessie. Did you have a request?"

"You didn't listen."

Tony watched her face as she relived the phone call. An unusual mix of anger and trepidation darkened her eyes, much as it had when the call had actually come in.

"*Who . . . who is this?*" she asked.

"*I had a request last week, Jessie. You ignored it. So let's try it again. Stay away from him.*"

"*S-stay away from who?*"

"*Falcone. Stay away from him, or he's going to get hurt.*"

Tony hit the stop button. "Did you catch that? Not '*you're* going to get hurt,' but '*he's* going to get hurt.' He's definitely threatening me."

"And I'm supposed to feel good about that?"

Her normally low voice was almost shrill, a clear sign that she was running on nerves now. Nerves that were raw and stretched to the limit.

"No," he said gently. "*I'm* supposed to feel relieved. At least a little bit. You may be the target of his attention, but I'm the target of his anger."

She lowered her head to her hands, raking her hair back from her face with widespread fingers. "I can't believe this is happening."

He couldn't either. And if he ever got his hands on the lunatic who was scaring her, he'd put an end to his ugly game swiftly and decisively.

"Look, Jess, while I don't think we can discount this as a problem, let's not give it too much credence either. It could just be a kid getting his jollies. We may even have heard the last of him tonight."

He didn't believe that, and when she lifted her head, he could see in her eyes that she didn't either.

"In the meantime," he went on, "let's come up

with some precautions we can take to keep him from getting too close, okay? Let's start with your home phone. Is the number listed under Fox?"

Her face went a whiter shade of pale at the realization that she might be vulnerable to this man in her own home.

Tony swore and was halfway around the table to her when she relaxed noticeably, drawing in a deep breath.

"Actually," she said, "my phone number is unlisted. It was a precaution I felt I should take when I moved here. You know, woman alone in a strange city. Made sense at the time." She shuddered. "Makes more sense now."

At least that was something, Tony thought as he leaned against the table, just within touching distance. Then he realized they had another problem.

"Those personalized Missouri license plates are going to have to go."

Her eyes widened. A small, sharp laugh burst out. "God. I feel like a target with a big bull's-eye on my back. If he wants to, he can reach me anywhere." She looked up at him. "And you're not any safer."

"He's not going to reach you, Jess." He'd make damn sure of that. "To get to you, he's going to have to come through me. And quite frankly I welcome the opportunity."

He was deadly calm, dead serious, but he didn't want to upset her more. "Like I said, we're probably getting excited about nothing. It's just some joker getting his jollies knowing he's frightening you. But to be on the safe side, I think we need to let the police in on this. I've got a friend on the force. I'll check with him first thing in the morning. Between us we'll figure out what to do."

Pocketing the tapes, he urged her to her feet. "Come on. You're beat. I'll walk you to your car, then follow you home."

She wanted to protest. He could see it was on the tip of her tongue to do so. But he could also see that she was weaving-on-her-feet tired and as tightly wound as a spring.

"This is not open for debate, Jess. We're leaving. Together. I'm pulling rank. Consider it boss's orders."

She stopped and made her position clear. "I won't let him run my life, Tony."

He almost smiled. That inner strength he'd sensed the first time he'd met her was back. She'd absorbed, weighed, considered, and made a decision. He believed her. She was too strong to let this get her down. But he'd be damned if he was going to let her deal with it on her own.

"He's not going to run your life. Or mine. We'll make sure of it. Now, come on. Just for tonight let me see that you get home okay. Friend to friend, all right?"

In control again, she smiled sheepishly. "When you put it that way, it wouldn't be very gracious of me to turn you down."

He opened the production-room door. "That was the idea."

"I never realized you were such a manipulative person."

He smiled. "Lady, there are a lot of things you don't know about me."

All that was about to change, though, he thought as they walked across the parking lot. Since Saturday night he'd had to balance and weigh the negatives against the positives of entering into a relationship with Jessie.

He had thought that given a little distance from her, the intensity of the feelings she evoked in him would fade. The old "out of sight, out of mind" theory would come into play. Considering the anticipation he'd felt both yesterday and today at the thought of seeing her, he knew he'd just been blowing smoke on that one.

Less, in Jessie's case, had simply left him wanting more. Much more. She did that to a man. She did it to him, at any rate. He didn't know where this was going, but he knew he wanted to take it further than he'd ever taken any relationship before. In a way it was a relief. He'd begun to buy in to the womanizer reputation he didn't deserve but was a popular misconception about him. He knew now that the fact of the matter was, until Jessie he simply hadn't been motivated to look beyond the here and now.

Suddenly, because of her he was eager to make that leap. And had he thought he would be doing her more good than harm, he'd have pressed for more that night. As it was, she didn't need another source of tension to compound the stress this telephone crazy had engendered.

The drive to her apartment was uneventful. So was the walk to her door. After Tony checked every nook and cranny of her apartment—convincing her to let him do it so that *he* could sleep that night—he resigned himself to leaving her alone. He had his hand on the doorknob, but stopped dead when the phone rang.

It screamed into the silence like an alarm.

Adrenaline fueled his actions. Adrenaline and the instinctual fear that filled her eyes. He bolted to the phone in three long strides, picking it up on the second ring.

"Hello." His voice was terse, tense.

Silence, then a hesitant, "I—I'm sorry. I must have the wrong number."

He breathed a huge sigh of relief. "No, wait, Sarah. Don't hang up. Your mother's right here."

With a sheepish look and a shrug of apology, he handed Jessie the receiver.

Cupping his palm around the back of his neck, he walked to the window, cursing his stupidity. She'd already told him her phone number was unlisted. The call had to have been from family or friend. The only thing his macho reaction had accomplished was to sharpen the edge she was already feeling.

Jessie waited until she'd composed herself before speaking. "Hi, sweetie. What's up?"

"Where've you been, Mom? I've been calling for the last hour."

Only then did Jessie notice the flashing light on her answering machine, indicating there were messages waiting.

"I'm sorry, Sarah. I ended up staying a little late after the show. We had some . . ." From the corner of her eye she saw Tony turn toward her, all his interest focused on what she was going to say. ". . . some material to go over for a promo that has to air in the morning."

While that seemed to mollify her daughter, the short silence that followed was a warning of Sarah's next question.

"Was that Tony who answered?"

Sarah didn't ask *why* Tony had answered the phone. She didn't have to. The question sailed across the lines like telepathy.

"Yes, it was Tony. I—I had brought some commercial copy home with me to work on over the weekend and forgot to bring it to the studio today. He's meeting with the client first thing in the morning and wants to take it with him. He just happened to be by the phone when I was at my desk digging up the folder."

She turned her back on Tony's amused grin, seeing in his eyes his appreciation for her fast mental footwork. "Honey, why are you calling so late? Is something wrong?"

"Nothing's wrong. I just wanted to tell you the show was great tonight. That's all. When I couldn't get you, and when you didn't call back, I got a little worried."

Jessie couldn't help but smile. "Tell me one thing, would you? When was it that *you* became the mother and *I* became the daughter? I'm supposed to worry about you, not the other way around. And speaking of worrying, what are you doing up so late on a school night?"

"I'm pulling an all-nighter. Big exam Wednesday and my first class tomorrow isn't until noon. So it's okay, okay?"

"Okay," Jessie said softly. "Just don't make a habit of it. You need your sleep. Regular hours wouldn't hurt either."

The following silence told her there was more on her daughter's mind.

"Sarah . . . what is it?"

"I—I was just wondering if you'd given any more thought to Dad is all."

She could have played dumb. She could have sidestepped. Neither ploy would have been fair to Sarah, though. "Honey, I don't want you holding out any hope on that count. I'm sorry that things haven't worked out for your father. But please remember, the choice was his. Our lives have been altered because of it. I don't want to look back. I don't want to *go* back. Not now. It was too hard getting here."

Sarah's silence cut deeply.

"I'm sorry, baby. I know you'd like things to be like they used to be, but it's just not going to happen.

"You okay?" she asked after another heartbreaking silence.

"Yeah, I'm okay. And I understand. I just . . . I don't know. I guess when he started making noises like he wanted to see you again, I had this silly notion that it might make everything all right." A long pause followed. "I know how much he hurt you, Mom. And I know how hard it's been for you to keep that hurt from affecting me. I won't bug you about it anymore, okay?"

"Thanks, sweetie." Jessie's heart swelled with pride, and with pain for crushing Sarah's hopes. "You know what? I'm going to miss our mother-daughter talks. But I can see our woman-to-woman talks are going to be even better."

"Woman to woman. I like that."

"Me too. And now, woman to woman, you get some rest, you hear?"

"Ditto. You work too hard. G'night."

"G'night, Sarah."

Jessie gently cradled the receiver, feeling both a loss and a fullness that filled her heart and brought the bittersweet sting of tears to her eyes.

"She seems like a very special young lady," Tony said from behind her.

Jessie turned to him, a reflective smile on her lips. "She's not my baby anymore. She's all grown up. At least she's getting there."

"And she'd like to see you and her father get back together." He shrugged guiltily. "Sorry. Couldn't miss the gist of the conversation. So he wants you back."

No apology there, Jessie mused. Just a straight-forward probe.

She hugged her arms around her waist. "So it seems."

"Can't say as I blame him."

She smiled tightly, determined not to look at him. "Once I would have jumped at the second chance."

"And now?"

Something about the hesitancy in his tone broke her resolve, and she met his eyes. They were intense, watchful. "And now it's not even a remote possibility."

She tried to tell herself it wasn't satisfaction she read on his face, but it was. Satisfaction and relief. And something more. A proprietary gleam that hinted at thoughts not fully developed but definitely far along in the planning stages.

"That's good," he said slowly. "Because I'd hate to lose you to him. I'd really hate it a lot."

Before she could decide if she was shocked or excited or in denial or all three, he smiled that coy, teasing smile of his and had her guessing again.

"After all, good employees are hard to find. Good copywriters even harder. And it goes without saying, the Fox is irreplaceable."

He brushed his fingertips across her cheek, then settled a hand lightly yet possessively on her shoulder. "You going to be okay now?"

Okay? Not likely. Not in this lifetime. Not with him looking at her that way.

"I could stay . . ."

She shook her head. No, he couldn't. Not and keep their employer-employee relationship intact. And that was all he was talking about. Wasn't it?

"I'm all right," she said.

"Right. That's why you're shaking."

He was implying that the caller was responsible. He was wrong. Tony's nearness, his scent, the memory of his arms around her and his mouth making love to hers Saturday night were the cause of her trembling.

It would be so easy to let it happen again. So easy to ask him to stay. Now and always, though, it would be wrong.

His other hand had found a home on her opposite shoulder and began a soothing massage. "And tense. My God, you're tense."

"Occupational hazard," she said, and tried to think through the rush of blood pounding in her ears and the heat of his big hands burning through the silk of her blouse. "And maybe a little fatigued. It's been a long day."

His hands stilled. "Translated: 'Would you get the hell out of my apartment so I can get some rest?'"

He had a way about him that constantly drew out her smile. "Translated: 'Thanks for seeing me home, and I think we both need to call it a day.'"

She didn't dare look at him. She focused instead

on that glistening silver falcon nestled in the silky dark curls at the base of his throat—and became fascinated with the way it seemed to shimmer with a life of its own. Then she got lost in remembering how instead of feeling cool against her fingers it had hummed with the warmth it had absorbed from his body.

His body. Solid. Strong. Muscled yet lean. All male. All temptation. All wrong.

She closed her eyes and prayed one of them would have the strength to escape the sensual web that was spinning around them and that she could no longer insist was one-sided.

She hadn't wanted to believe it. She hadn't let herself believe it, not at first. But it was true. If the way his broad hands swept down her back and pulled her close was any indication, he wanted her.

She swallowed hard and raised her gaze to his.

"Because I care, Jess, I'm leaving you alone tonight."

He brushed the hair back from her face, his fingers lingering, then dropping to cup her nape. His eyes softened with a telltale arousal that he'd banked in favor of her need.

"Because I care," he continued, "you need to know up front that the time will come when we will talk about this. About what I feel for you. About what you feel for me."

Her hands rose to clutch his wrists, whether to push him away or hold him close she no longer knew. "Tony . . ."

"Because I care," he went on softly, "I want you to know that the night will come when I won't leave you."

She trembled, and he touched his mouth to her hair. "Lock up tight. Get some rest. I'll see you in the morning."

After a fierce, possessive embrace, he turned and headed out the door.

Like a man with his tail on fire, she thought, watching him go.

Like a man who had exercised the last of his restraint in willing himself to leave her.

And she, like a fool, could only stand there, smiling as if she had good sense, and dizzy with longing.

Jessie wasn't smiling the next morning.

She pried an eye open, squinted at her alarm, saw that it was not yet six A.M., and pulled a pillow over her ears to block out the hammering sound.

It didn't work. By the time she'd tossed the pillow aside, along with her covers, she'd finally realized that the ringing she'd thought was her alarm was in fact her doorbell. The hammering was someone pounding on her door.

She shrugged into her short pink chenille robe, stumbled across the living room, and peeked through the hole.

Ramming back the dead bolt, she flipped the security lock and yanked open the door.

"You just left," she accused with a morning-gruff growl.

Tony stood in the hall, beaming, bright-eyed, and laughing at her. "I love it. Who would have thought that the sweetheart of KXAL was not a morning person?"

"I'm not a *person* in the morning," she corrected him emphatically. "I am a troll. And you, Tony Falcone, are in deep dirt. I eat obnoxiously cheerful Italians for breakfast."

His eyes, all sass and innuendo, sparkled with invitation. "If you insist."

She growled, left him standing in the doorway, and trudged to the bathroom, slamming the door behind her.

Thirty minutes later, showered, dressed for work in a mauve shirtwaist and with a light application of makeup that she hoped covered the damage of a night short on sleep and long on turmoil, she joined him in the kitchen.

He'd made himself comfortable. Perched on a tall stool at the breakfast island, he looked like he always looked—casual, relaxed, unconsciously sexy in black pleated slacks and a lightweight olive-green sweater with the sleeves pushed up on his powerfully muscled forearms.

He also looked like he thought he belonged in her kitchen and that she should get used to waking up and finding him there. Unsettling as that notion was, it was even more upsetting that she found herself liking the idea.

"I made myself at home," he said, watching her carefully as he slid a cup of coffee her way. "I hope it's the way you like it."

The coffee smelled wonderful. So did he. She wrapped her hands around the mug, needing something to steady herself, and inhaled the delicious aroma. "You scored major points with this one, Falcone."

"Then this ought to score me even higher." He reached behind him and set a plate of glazed croissants between them. "Enjoy."

As breezy as his smile was that morning, he didn't fool her. Not for a minute.

"I know what you're doing."

"Doing?" he asked easily.

"I don't need a bodyguard, Falcone. And I don't need a baby-sitter."

"What do you need, Jess?"

Laden with invitation, the words hung between them like the steam rising from her mug. She raised her eyes to his, telling herself she was prepared for his playful grin, that in the sparkling light of morning she could handle it.

He wasn't grinning, though. And his look wasn't playful.

It was open and searching, sincere and seeking. And for an instant before his smile took over, it was so poignantly vulnerable, it was all she could do to keep from reaching across the counter and touching him.

He cared about her. He cared *for* her. This man,

who could have any woman he wanted, wanted her. In that brief moment his eyes had betrayed the doubt that she might not want him back.

"What do you need, Jess?" he repeated softly. "Tell me and it's yours."

Well, there it was, she thought, out in the open. No more sidestepping around the issue. She knew he wanted her, and he was asking what it would take to have her.

She wanted him too. She could see in his eyes that he knew it. The only thing left open for debate was what she was going to do about it.

She pinched her eyes shut and exhaled the breath she hadn't been aware she'd been holding.

"Time," she said finally, not at all certain when she'd decided to open herself up to something that now seemed inevitable, and overwhelmed by the knowledge that she just had.

"I need time, Tony," she restated quietly, and prayed to God she hadn't opened a door that should never have been unlocked.

"Time to consider us?"

The huskiness of his voice touched her. She nodded.

"Together. As lovers. As much much more than friends."

The room seemed to pulse to the rhythm of her heart. When she found the courage to look at him, his eyes had softened and darkened. The promises she saw in them stole what little resistance she'd been harboring.

"Yes," she said. Hearing the breathlessness in her own voice, she steadied her hands by tightening her grip on the mug.

"Then it's time that I'll give you, Jess. All the time you need."

Just as swiftly, however, his face became shadowed again. "I wish I could make the same promise for my friend, Tom."

She raised her head, her brow furrowed. "Your friend Tom?"

"He's the one I told you about who's on the police force. He's agreed to meet with us this morning."

A long moment passed while she made herself deal with the fact that her attraction to Tony Falcone and her decision to act on that attraction was not her only problem. Nor was it the most pressing.

"I'm sorry," he said, a grim twist to his mouth. "I'm sorry you have to deal with this. I'm sorry I had to remind you. But I don't think we should put it off any longer. If you're finished with your coffee, we'd better get going."

Feeling as grim as he sounded, she nodded and slipped away from the counter.

She wanted to put it off. She wanted to forget about it. But the fact was it wasn't going to go away. She walked to the bedroom to get her purse, then, reluctant but resolute, she headed for the door.

SIX

Tony had met Tom Wayfield when KXAL had hosted a benefit for the San Diego Police Department's Benevolent Association. What had started out as a business relationship had turned into a comfortable friendship. Close to Tony's age, a family man, the stocky, crew-cut blond police detective instilled confidence and trust. Tony had liked him the moment he'd met him. And while it had been a couple of months since they'd abused each other, both verbally and physically, with a friendly session on the racketball court, Tony knew he could count on Tom.

As he sat opposite Tom in Tom's office, however, talking across a desk littered with paperwork, Tony couldn't say he much cared for what his friend had to say. Not all of it, at any rate.

"Stalker?" Tony repeated, disbelief and denial threaded through the word in equal measures.

The detective glanced apologetically at Jessie,

tossed the cassettes they'd just listened to onto his desk, and leaned back in his chair.

"I'm just covering all bases," he said diplomatically. "You came here with a problem. I'm speculating on the possibilities."

"And you think a stalker is a possibility."

Tom laced his hands behind his head and sighed. "Two phone calls do not a stalker make. Two phone calls make a pest. An annoyance. A royal pain in the butt who gets his jollies scaring people. It could just be a power trip for this guy. And it's a real possibility that next week someone else will be the target of his little game."

Tony leaned forward in the wooden chair and propped his elbows on his knees. "So what can you do?"

"Nothing. Not at this point. Neither of you can identify the voice. Without an ID, we're dead in the water."

"What do you suggest we do?" Jessie asked, sounding anxious and tired.

"Go home," Tom said kindly. "Go on about your business. You may never hear from him again."

"And if we do?"

"If you do, try to keep him on the phone longer. Maybe something will come to you. You might even recognize the voice."

Tony watched as the color drained from Jessie's face.

"You're suggesting it might be someone I know?"

she asked in a small voice that relayed how resistant she was to that idea.

Tom shrugged. "It's a possibility. A slim one. More than likely, though, it's someone who feels they know you through the radio. If he keeps calling, the pattern usually follows that eventually he'll want you to know who he is. Most stalkers drop little hints, make it a point to lead you on. Sometimes they'll come right out and identify themselves."

"And that's when you can do something," she said.

Tom blew out a big breath. "Not necessarily."

"Come on, Tom." Tony shot out of the chair, hands on hips. "Are you saying even if we give you this guy, you can't do anything?"

"Look. I appreciate your frustration, but there has to be implied intent, a credible threat of bodily harm."

"You heard the tape," Jessie said. "He said Tony was going to get hurt if I didn't stay away from him."

"But he was talking to you. He was not threatening *you*. And quite frankly we'd have a hard time proving that was actually a threat. It could imply that you are the one who's going to hurt him."

Tony swore. "This is incredible."

Tom gave another helpless shrug. "I'm sorry. I know this isn't what you want to hear."

"You're damn right," Tony muttered, feeling as edgy as a caged bear and twice as mean. "It's not at all what I want to hear."

"It's probably not much consolation, but the latest studies indicate there are approximately two hundred thousand people in the United States alone —particularly women—who are being stalked by someone. Celebrities lead the list. Like it or not, you two are celebrities now—at least you are in San Diego. While it's frightening, the upside is that it's rare that anyone actually gets hurt."

"Rare, but not never?" Jessie asked, and Tony could see in her eyes that she really didn't want to hear the answer.

Tom conceded with a nod. "I'm sorry I can't help. In the meantime try to go on with business as usual. You may never hear from him again. If you do, remember what I said. Try to keep him on the line longer and get him on tape again."

He rose and walked them to the door. "Keep in touch, okay? And Tony," he added in a hushed voice, making sure Jessie was out of earshot, "watch your back. If this thing mushrooms, put that macho Italian adrenaline of yours on hold and get in touch with me. Don't try to be a hero."

Hero, Tony thought grimly, as he walked with Jessie down the hall, his hand settled lightly but protectively at the small of her back. He'd never been a hero. At least not when it counted. He'd never been put to the test. Sure, his high school football-star status had carried over to Stanford, where he'd been the "hero" of more than one game. His good hands and fast feet had even had the pros courting him. And while a chronic shoulder injury had been a deterrent to a career in the NFL, it hadn't been the deciding factor. He'd simply outgrown the game.

What was happening here was not a game. What was happening here was ugly. And as he walked Jessie across the cracked asphalt parking lot to his car, aware of the stiffness in her shoulders, of her slight frame and ultimate vulnerability, that macho Italian adrenaline Tom was concerned about surged through his blood like a Patriot missile.

Hero? Where Jessie was concerned, heroics weren't an issue. The simple fact was that he'd do anything and everything in his power to protect her. In his book that didn't make him a hero, only a man concerned about his woman.

Jessie left the police department in a daze, wishing she'd wake up and find this was all a bad dream. The indisputable fact, however, was that it was far too real.

After they were settled into Tony's car and he'd pulled out into the street, she forced herself to regroup and consider everything Tom Wayfield had said. He was the expert, and in all likelihood he was right. This guy was just a prankster. He'd get bored and turn his attention to some other poor, unfortunate someone until he tired of that game, too, and on and on.

She wanted to believe it. She was determined to try—until she realized Tony was heading in a direction opposite from the station.

"Where are we going?"

"DMV," he answered. "We're getting those license plates changed today. You're a California girl now, Jess. It's time to fly your new colors."

She felt a tug of tenderness toward him and his attempt to cover his reasons for wanting to get her plates changed. Beneath his show of casualness Tony wasn't as convinced as his friend that this wasn't a dangerous game they'd been recruited to play.

"And when we finish there," he added as he made a left turn, "we have a little more business to take care of."

"Business? What business? I'm drawing a blank."

"I think I'll let Brian tell you about it."

Something in his voice, a protracted hesitance, an overriding inflection of guilt, had her brow creased in a frown.

"Why do I get the feeling I'm not going to like what this business is?"

He immediately looked sheepish, confirming her suspicions, but he refused to talk about it, saying only that Brian would fill her in.

It took well over an hour for Jessie to register as a California driver and get her new driver's license and license plates. When she and Tony finally reached the radio station, she headed straight for Brian's office, refusing to wait any longer to find out what "business" Tony had been talking about. Brian seemed startled to see them, then waved them both into chairs. Jessie opened her mouth to ask what was going on, but Brian forestalled her.

"I've scheduled another photo shoot," he said hesitantly.

Jessie leaned back in her chair, closed her eyes, and groaned. She'd known it was coming. She just hadn't thought it would be so soon. And what with this caller business, she'd pushed it to the back of her mind.

She opened her eyes. "When?"

Brian's gaze darted from her to Tony, then back to her before the pen in his hands became the focus of his attention. "Well, that's the tough part. I've got a crew lined up for this afternoon."

"This afternoon?" A little curl of anxiety tightened to a knot in her chest.

He shrugged, looking more and more uncomfortable. "I'm sorry I couldn't give you more warning."

She snorted. "I'll bet."

While Brian sat there looking guilty, Tony tried to charm her with a grin. It almost worked, because in spite of his duplicity she was relieved to see him smile. It was the first one she'd seen since they'd entered Tom Wayfield's office at nine-fifteen that morning.

"You knew about this, didn't you?" she said to him. His silence confirmed her accusation. "You are a very sneaky man. And you," she went on, facing Brian again, "you intended to spring this on me on purpose so I wouldn't have time to think about it and say no."

"I know it looks that way," Brian said, "but the honest truth is that it really did come up in a hurry. It just sort of worked out that way. You know how it goes. We're relying a lot on calling in favors to keep the budget down. Kent—You remember Kent, don't you?"

Kent Newman was a hard man to forget, Jessie thought. Something about the photographer who had shot them as Scarlett and Rhett had set the hair on the back of her neck on end. She'd never pinpointed exactly what it was that bothered her. It could have been the penetrating blue of his eyes, the razor-sharp cut of his profile. It could have been his intensity. Or his ability to read her thoughts and draw unwanted emotions from her.

His photographs were evidence of that. He had captured every sexual spark arcing between her and Tony. It was a little frightening to know that a stranger could read her so well.

And that same stranger, armed with his Hasselblad and a wide-angle lens, was going to have the opportunity to draw those responses out of her again.

"Yes, I remember Kent," she said softly.

"He had a cancellation, so he was able to work us right in," Brian said. "If we don't take advantage, it's hard telling when he'll be available again."

"Oh, well," she groused sarcastically, "far be it from us not to take advantage."

Tony's smile suddenly vanished, and a scowl darkened his face. "I don't know," he said, almost to himself, then caught Jessie's eye. "Maybe we ought to call it off."

She knew what he was thinking. It had nothing to

do with her discomfort over appearing on another billboard and everything to do with their mysterious caller and the threat he represented in their lives.

Brian frowned as he watched the exchange between them. "Is there something going on here that I should know about?"

She held Tony's gaze, then responded to his unasked question with a nod.

"Yeah," Tony said, turning to Brian and exhaling a deep breath. "There's something going on. I guess it's time we fill you in."

Brian's frown deepened as Tony told him about the calls, the threats, and the fear that they might be dealing with a stalker.

"Oh, man," he said after Tony was through. "You don't have any idea who it is?"

"Not a clue."

Brian turned to Jessie, his kind face full of concern. "Jessie—are you okay?"

She smiled. "Yes. It's just frustrating."

"And frightening, I'd guess," he added, walking around his desk to sit on the edge of it, directly in front of her. "Maybe Tony's right. Maybe we should forget about the shoot."

"No," Jessie heard herself saying. She met Brian's gaze, then turned to Tony, full of fire and purpose. "Like I said, I'm not going to let this guy run my life. We go on about our business. We do the shoot. And we do it as scheduled today."

"You're sure you want to do this?" Tony asked, offering her another opportunity to put it off.

She drew in a determined breath. "I'm sure I want to do this."

She did not want to do this!

She did not want to do this in the worst way.

She'd thought Scarlett and Rhett had been bad. She'd thought she'd had it whipped when she'd nixed Tarzan and Jane. Well, the lord and lady of the jungle didn't hold a candle to what Brian had planned for them today.

The replica of Cleopatra's barge heaved with the illusion of floating on the flowing waters of the Nile. Jessie stood before it and closed her eyes—but not too tightly. She didn't want to spoil the makeup it had taken Clarice Klein—KXAL's full-time receptionist, part-time budding makeup artist—nearly an hour to get just right.

"I'm amazing!" Clarice declared, her brown eyes dancing as she looked Jessie up and down for any detail she might have missed. A huge smile split her mahogany-colored face. "If the original Cleopatra had looked as good back then as you look right now, girl, she never would have done herself in with that asp. You are a fiiinnnne sight."

Jessie wished she could share Clarice's enthusiasm. She also wished she could argue with Clarice about her appearance, but Clarice was right. She was a sight. In fact, Jessie decided, as she made her way across the small stage and tried to figure out the best way to board the barge without drawing too much attention to herself, she was a spectacle.

Her costume—which she considered better suited to a harem slave girl than a queen of Egypt—revealed quite a bit of cleavage and midriff. Drifts of peek-a-boo white silk alternately covered and exposed long lengths of leg. Try as she might to ignore it, Jessie knew that every person on the set was watching her.

Kent, his long blond hair tied back with an ice-blue bandanna that matched his eyes, called for more light as he checked angle after angle with his light meter.

"I think we're set here," he announced to the room in general. After a long, thoroughly disconcerting assessment of Jessie in her costume, makeup, and black wig, he looked around for Tony. "Do you suppose we could get Antony out here? I don't want to offend his Roman sensibilities, but we've got to wrap this up in a little over two hours. Our gracious thespians aren't going to take kindly to the barge being occupied at curtain time."

As far as Jessie was concerned, two hours in front of Kent and his camera was two hours too long. Still, small favors being what they were, she was thankful they weren't looking at an all-day shoot.

Brian had found the little theater where a local acting troupe was currently performing *Antony and Cleopatra*. Since they had allowed Brian the use of costumes, stage sets, and props, even Jessie had to admit it was a golden opportunity for the next classic-couple reenactment.

She also had to admit that if she'd known about the skimpiness of her costume, she'd be home at that very moment, locked in the closet of her choice.

She threw Brian an "I'll deal with you later" glare. His guilty look didn't escape her as he quickly became busy consulting with one of the lighting technicians.

You ought to feel guilty, she thought. And she should have known better than to agree to this. But it was too late for hindsight now. Especially when the commotion behind her indicated Antony had arrived. She turned to see him, and figured it just might be too late for a lot of things.

As Scarlett's Rhett, Tony had taken her breath away.

As Cleopatra's Antony, he stole her power of speech as well.

Grinning a grin made all the more engaging because Tony was obviously a little uncomfortable with his own costume, he held his arms wide for appraisal.

"Well, what do you think? Is it me?"

It was him, Jessie thought. It was definitely him.

It was almost more of him than she could handle with an audience standing by.

"Holy Roman oracle," Clarice whispered in awe behind her. "Did you ever see the like?"

No, Jessie thought dismally. She never. And if she made it through this day without embarrassing herself, she hoped she'd never "see the like" again. At least not with all these people looking on.

His beautiful head of raven-black hair was haloed

with a crown of myrtle. The pure-white toga that left one shoulder and half of his chest bare, ended at the top of his powerfully muscled thighs. The skimpy drape of fabric left little to the imagination and an abundance of sculpted muscle and rippling bronze skin to drool over.

"All right, people, let's get this barge afloat, what do you say?"

Jessie snapped her gaze to Kent, who, with an arm draped over his camera, was waiting impatiently for some cooperation.

"Or were you two going to compare togas all afternoon?"

"Brian, you owe me for this," Tony grumbled good-naturedly as he cupped Jessie's elbow and helped her onto the barge. "The last time I wore a bedsheet in public, I was young enough to be excused and drunk enough not to care."

"Until this moment," she said, settling gingerly onto the ornate black damask lounge that she would share with Tony, "I would have sworn that neither would have done the trick for me."

He chuckled. "I believe it's called stretching our limits."

"I believe it's called temporary insanity."

"That works for me," Tony said easily. "Defense attorneys have gotten their clients off murder raps with less motive."

"Does that mean no jury in the world will convict me when I wring Brian's neck tomorrow?"

"I don't know if I'd take it quite that far."

"And I didn't know he'd take this billboard business quite this far. Tony—"

"Hey," Kent interrupted. "Do you suppose we could get a little cooperation here?"

Brian evidently had experienced a late-breaking and overwhelming surge of guilt. "Jessie," he said from the foot of the stage, "we can still call it off if you're too uncomfortable."

Tony gave her a searching look. She was tempted. But she was also a professional, and professionals took the bad lumps along with the good licks.

"Let's just get it over with."

Tony squeezed her arm in encouragement, then turned his attention to Kent. "We're set when you are. Just tell us how you want us to pose."

Kent approached them, considering the lounge and the lighting. "I've got an idea."

Jessie didn't like the look in his eyes.

By the time he'd positioned them the way he wanted them, she understood why.

Tony had to hand it to Kent. He knew how to stage a seduction. First he had Jessie semirecline on the lounge. Then he positioned one of her feet on the floor, the other on the lounge. With both knees bent at forty-five-degree angles, the soft folds of shimmering silk drifted free, exposing the beautiful length of her long, supple legs.

And that was only the beginning. Kent then posed Tony above her, one foot also on the floor so that his bare leg flanked hers. The knee of his other leg sank into the black damask lounge between her thighs.

"Now, bend over her," Kent instructed. "Use the near camera arm to hold you both free of the lounge and band the off camera arm around her, just below her shoulder blades. Yes. Like that. Good.

"Now draw her toward you. Wrap those fingers wide. I want to see them just below her breast. Good, that's good," Kent exclaimed, as Tony's hold caused Jessie to arch her back and unintentionally thrust her breasts against his chest.

He felt a tremor shudder through her at the moment of contact. Their eyes met and held, telling of the sensual awareness of the softness of her breasts and the swift hardening of her nipples. Another tremor, electric with that awareness, followed on the heels of the first one—only this time he wasn't sure which one of them was having trouble with control.

"Jessie," Kent said, drawing them both back to the business at hand. "Let your head fall back. Yes, just like that. Now let your eyes drift shut. More . . . more . . . there. Stop, that's perfect. And now your mouth. Wet your lips and keep them parted."

The look of her, the feel of her beneath him, the hunger that had grown to a gnawing ache inside him, almost proved too much for Tony. Her parted lips were an erotic invitation for him to order everyone off the set and bring this scene to a conclusion that had nothing to do with revenue and everything to do with desire.

"Perfect," Kent pronounced, his voice reminding Tony of the presence of their audience.

"Whatever you do, you two, don't move. Don't even breathe." Satisfied with his handiwork, Kent stepped back behind the camera and began shooting. "If this turns out the way I think it will, I'll have to invest in a pair of asbestos gloves just to handle the negatives."

And if he had to hold her in this pose for the next two hours, Tony thought, trying to concentrate on anything but the feel of her skin beneath his hand, the subtle scent she wore that teased and tormented his senses, he was going to embarrass himself in front of God and everyone.

Fortunately Kent did reposition them a few times, and none of the subsequent poses were as erotic as the first. Still, they were both shaking by the time Kent finished shooting. The exertion of a hard-fought battle with his self-control was the reason Tony was feeling so shaky. He suspected from the tentative way Jessie was looking at him as they drew apart that her reason for trembling ran in tandem with his.

Every erogenous zone in his body was charged with awareness of her scent, of her silken heat, of the desire that shimmered in her eyes and his escalating need to satisfy it.

The little theater was unaccountably quiet, as if everyone on the set sensed the electricity between them. Even Clarice was unusually reserved as Tony and Jessie negotiated the barge and walked off the stage. Brian looked downright embarrassed. Kent was scowling as he broke down his equipment and stowed it away.

In silence they went to their respective dressing rooms to remove costumes and makeup.

"Well," Tony said, watching Jessie's face to gauge her reaction when they met again at the stage door. "That was a little intense."

"*Intense* is a good word," she agreed.

"I'm sorry it made you uncomfortable."

She shrugged. "It's over."

Yes, the shoot was over, but as he'd known since the night he'd brought her home in the rain, what was happening between them had just begun. Whenever he was with her, every time they touched, an escalating awareness that was charged with anticipation and rich with promise took over.

He'd never been this tuned to the needs of a woman. He'd never experienced this consuming desire to fulfill those needs.

He supposed he should have seen it coming. His friends had been telling him that one day the woman would come along who would shake his tree but good and have him reassessing his confirmed-bachelor status. Not only had he not believed them, he hadn't known the feelings would be so strong.

And he hadn't expected that the woman would come equipped with a daughter and a stalker. Neither had he known that he'd harbored such protective instincts all these years. Maybe because those same instincts took him so off guard, he could be excused for what happened when they arrived at her apartment and he spotted the single red rose lying in front of her door.

He watched as, hesitant and wary, she bent over and picked it up. Slowly she unfolded the note attached to the stem and read it.

She handed the note to Tony, then closed her eyes and slumped against the apartment door.

He read it in silence.

Does he give you roses?

"I don't suppose you have any idea who would have left this?" he asked, forcing a calm he was far from feeling.

"I don't suppose I do."

She looked at him then, her eyes pleading as she struggled against the conclusion they were both reluctant to draw. "It's from him, isn't it?"

He clenched his jaw and looked away. He'd like to deny it, but every instinct he possessed agreed with her. "It would seem we've gone from threats to competition."

"And it would seem he knows where I live."

That was the worst part, Tony knew. He was way too close for comfort.

Squeezing her hand between his, he took the key from her cold fingers, slipped it into the lock, and swung open the door. After a quick look around he motioned her inside.

"Come on. It's okay."

She slumped onto the sofa, the long-stemmed rose dangling limply from her hand. "It's not okay.

It's not going to be okay until we find out who is doing this and why."

Relieving her of the rose and the note, he stuffed the rose down the garbage disposal and the note into his pocket to take to Tom Wayfield. The doorbell rang just as he was about to join her on the sofa.

Her gaze shot to his, full of apprehension, shadowed with fear. In that instant he felt another surge of anger against whoever had placed that fear in her eyes.

"You were expecting someone?"

She shook her head.

He placed a finger to his lips and walked soundlessly to the door. When he checked the peephole and saw a man standing outside in the hall, he didn't stop to think about his actions. He jerked the door open, grabbed a handful of shirt, and dragged the man inside.

After kicking the door closed, Tony slammed the stranger face first against the wall and twisted his arm behind his back, holding him there.

When he groaned, Tony only shoved him harder.

"Who are you and what are you doing here?"

"For Pete's sake . . ." the man muttered, then groaned again as Tony increased the pressure on his arm. "W-what the . . . What are you doing?"

"I'm asking questions. And in another minute I'm going to be real upset that I'm not getting any answers. Now, who the hell are you?"

"Kyle," he managed between gritted teeth. "Kyle Sullivan. I'm a frie—"

"Oh, my God," Jessie said as she hurried up behind Tony and touched his arm. "Tony. Please. Let him go."

He glanced over his shoulder at her, never releasing the pressure. "You know him?"

"Not exactly. But I recognize his name. He's a friend of Sarah's."

Slowly, his adrenaline still flowing hot and thick and wild, Tony released the young man's arm. Slower still he backed a step away.

Rubbing his arm, his eyes wide and wary, Kyle turned to stare first at Tony, then at Jessie.

"Oh, Kyle," she said. "I'm so sorry. Are you all right?"

He flexed his shoulder and grimaced. "Yeah. I guess. But what the devil's going on?"

"There—there have been some break-ins in the neighborhood lately," she lied, sending Tony a silent warning not to dispute her.

Kyle scowled from Jessie to Tony, then looked back at Jessie again. "What kind of a thief rings a doorbell?"

Jessie glanced at Tony, silently asking him to field that question.

"Can you think of an easier way to get in?" Tony grumbled, trying to excuse his Hulk Hogan tactics by abetting Jessie's lie.

"I think maybe this was a case of overreacting," Jessie added apologetically.

While it was clear he wasn't convinced, Kyle shrugged and let it go. "Whatever."

"I'm sorry," Tony added belatedly. "Are you sure you're okay?"

"Yeah, I'm sure." Still, he eased a step away. "Sarah sent me over for the laptop."

"Right," Jessie said, forcing a smile. "I knew she needed it again. I'll just go get it.

"I'd appreciate it if you didn't say anything to Sarah about this, Kyle," she said when she returned to the room with the computer. "She worries. And I don't want her getting upset about the break-ins. Can you do that for me?"

Backing to the door, Kyle cast another skeptical glance Tony's way. "No problem."

"Kyle." Jessie placed a hand on his arm. "I really am sorry. I've been looking forward to meeting you. We'll try this again sometime, okay?"

"Yeah. Sure. Look . . . I've really got to go now."

Without another word he left.

"Burglar?" Tony asked, raising an eyebrow.

"I don't want Sarah to know about this stalker business."

"I understand." He was silent for some time before he shook his head in self-deprecation. "What I *don't* understand is that until I met you, I considered myself a pretty passive person."

She couldn't help but grin as she recalled how Kyle had scurried out the door to get away from them. "I'm sure Kyle will be glad to hear that—as soon as his arm quits hurting."

SEVEN

Jessie looked up from her desk to see Tony standing in her doorway. The sight had become far too familiar during the past week and a half, and she'd learned that the man had the persistence of a used-car salesman.

"Tony, this has got to stop."

"I don't know what you're talking about, Jess."

Innocence. He had the look down to an art form. Quite an accomplishment given the way he'd played "up against the wall" with poor Kyle last week. It was even more of a challenge to pull off with those Lucifer-black eyes of his, that hair that was too long and too thick, and that mouth, which tormented and teased and promised illicit pleasures.

Well, she wasn't going to let him win this round, no matter how innocent or appealing or mouth-wateringly gorgeous he looked.

She forced herself to focus on the middle of his

forehead as he leaned a shoulder against the door-frame, his chamois jacket hooked on a finger and slung over his other shoulder.

But the falcon glittered at his throat, beckoning her gaze to feast on the dark, silken curls peeking above the neckline of yet another of the V-neck sweaters he had a penchant for wearing and that looked so right on him. This one was the color of ivory, a soft contrast to the cinnamon-colored pleated slacks he wore with such unassuming grace.

With great effort she pried her gaze away. "You know exactly what I'm talking about, you walking, talking equivalent of an Italian steamroller. And I'm not letting you get away with it again. Go home. Do not walk me to my car. Do not follow me to my apartment. No," she insisted when he tried to break in. "No more manufactured reasons. My license plates are changed. The bumper sticker is gone. You did not leave your keys in my apartment. My front left tire does not look a little low. The extra security locks are in place, and I never open my door to a stranger. I can go home all by myself just like a big girl."

"Jess," he said patiently as he eased his tight, tidy tush onto a corner of her desk.

The man did not play fair.

She blew out a deep breath. "What?"

"I picked you up for work this morning, remember? You can't get home on your own steam because your car is in the garage being serviced."

She slowly counted to ten. "Smugness does not become you."

He crossed his arms over his chest and got comfortable. "You're cute as hell when you get in a snit."

"I do not get in snits," she said stiffly, getting into a fairly good imitation of one. "And don't call me cute."

"Did you know that smoke actually comes out of the top of your head when you get like this? And your ears—just the very tips, mind you—get as red as stop lights."

She grabbed her purse from her bottom desk drawer, slung the strap over her shoulder, and marched around her desk. "One more word and I'm calling a cab."

He shook his head and smiled at the floor. "My mother's going to love you."

That stopped her cold. All the steam whooshed out of her body. All of her confidence deserted her too. She stopped short with her hand clutching the doorknob.

Ten days had passed since she'd opened herself up to *thinking* about the possibility of entering into a relationship with him. Ten days, and as he had promised, he'd given her time. He hadn't pressed. Not that he hadn't kept her awareness level high. He did that just by existing. But he also made it clear—with a look that could melt her bones, or a touch too intimate to be casual, too lingering to be ignored—that his interest hadn't faded. If anything, she sensed his attraction was growing stronger. Hers was too.

Always in the background, though, like a dark shadow lurking between the present and the future, was the caller and the threat of his unknown motive.

He hadn't called again, and there hadn't been any more roses. They'd almost finished out another week of shows, and there'd been nothing. It was encouraging, but not enough to close the book. It was enough to keep her on edge, though. She didn't think much past the day-to-day workload at the station and Tony's not-so-subtle bodyguard ploys.

The mention of his mother, though, added a new dimension to the problems of the older-woman, younger-man scenario. Cold water couldn't have cooled her off more effectively.

He must have seen the withdrawal in her eyes.

"Hey," he said, slipping off her desk. He reached around her and shut her office door to the prying eyes of anyone who might wander by. Without preamble or apology he drew her into his arms. "My mother *is* going to love you."

"Right."

He shook her gently. "You're making way too much out of this."

The "this" he was referring to was their age difference, and it was the first time it had come out in the open.

"How old are you, Tony?" she asked point-blank.

"Old enough to know what I want when I see it. I want you, Jess. Every day. In every way."

As if putting it into words wasn't enough, he drew her closer, settling his hips against hers, taking her breath away at the strength of his arousal pressed against her belly.

"See what you do to me?" he whispered against her hair. "See how quickly I come alive when you're near? It's killing me, Jess. The wanting. The waiting."

"I'm sure your mother will be glad to hear that."

He groaned, then chuckled. "Nice try, but it won't work. You're not going to distract me. I've promised to give you time, and you've got it. All the time you need. But I've decided that while I'm waiting for you to make up your sweet mind, you need a little something extra to think about."

He nudged her hips again, then lowered his mouth to her ear and whispered in graphic, exquisite detail what he had planned for her the first time he got her in his bed.

One huge, engulfing wave of heat, desire, and wild longing swept her from breast to belly as she pictured what he so erotically described.

She swayed against him. "Does—does your mother know you talk like that?" she asked breathlessly.

He chuckled again, then, with a full body shiver, set her away from him. "I'm beginning to wish I'd never brought my mother into this conversation. Come on." He took her hand and opened the door. "I'm taking you to dinner. No arguments. No business talk. No stalker talk. Just you and me. Tonight you can ask anything your little heart desires about Tony Falcone, and I'll answer."

"Anything?"

"You got it."

"How old are you?" she asked as he led her out the door.

"Anything but that," he said with a grin.

Oh, Lord. It must be worse than she thought.

Tony took her to the Rusty Pelican. They sat in a quiet corner by the window overlooking the ocean and talked to the sound of the surf and the gulls playing among the breakers. Or at least she talked. That was fine with him. He could have listened to her forever.

When sunset brought darkness with it, they lingered over wine and watched the evening mellow out to the dancing flames from the fire pits on the beach.

"Why is it," she said as she skimmed a finger over the lip of her glass, "that we came here for me to learn about you and I ended up doing most of the talking?"

"Maybe I'm a good listener and you needed to talk," he suggested. "Maybe I find listening to you fascinating."

"Fascinating? Nothing about my life is fascinating. Like me, it's down-home, midwestern normal. I'm not sure what kept you from nodding off over your linguine."

"Fascinating," he insisted, thinking of some of the secrets she'd shared. Little things, like the fact that she favored her mother. That her dad still called her his little pumpkin. That she and her sister, Anna, used to share a room and listen to the radio into the wee hours, dreaming about the man behind the midnight voice of their favorite DJ. That she'd broken her wrist falling off her bike when she was nine.

Yup. Fascinating stuff. The tip of the proverbial iceberg. He just kept wanting more.

"And to think I felt guilty for accusing you of being manipulative the other night," she said with more amusement than reproach.

"*Manipulative* is a harsh word." He considered her over his wine and grinned. "I think I like *charming* better."

She dipped her head, conceding. "Definitely that. Charming, engaging, and utterly . . . beautiful," she added, almost regretfully. "Which leads to the obvious question. Tony . . ." She hesitated, then took the leap. "Why me?"

He knew what she was asking. Why not someone his own age?

"Why shouldn't it be you?"

"I'd think the overriding reasons would be obvious."

He leaned back, hooking an arm negligently over the back of his chair. "Enlighten me."

"I'm the one who needs to be enlightened here. I don't have a clue as to why you're interested in me. No, wait. Maybe I do and I just don't want to accept it."

He was silent for a moment, considering. "You think this is about sex, Jess?"

Firelight and moonglow shone through the huge plate-glass window. Together they played in harmony across her face, highlighting, caressing, showcasing her beauty and her concern.

"You think this is just a little curiosity tumble for me," he asked, "a sexual conquest, so to speak?"

She averted her gaze to the window and the fires outside. He was painfully aware that her silence relayed how often that thought had crossed her mind.

He swore, a soft but explicit expression of disgust. "I can't believe you listen to that crap. I can't believe you think that's what *I'm* all about."

He knew what people said about him. That every woman whose path he crossed ended up a notch on his bedpost. He wasn't particularly proud of it, but there had been a phase in his life when it might have been true. He'd been a very young man, and like most young men he had not been immune to the lure of beautiful women.

"Okay," he began reasonably. "Maybe I deserve some of this. Maybe I even brought some of it on myself. But don't hold me responsible for something that happened in my life years before I met you.

"Look, Jess. I know I've been coming on to you pretty strong. That's my mistake too. I want you, and I want you to know it. And I want a chance to try this relationship on for size."

She was quiet for a moment, staring out the window, at her wine, staring at anything but him. "And what if it doesn't fit? I'm not up to an affair, Tony. I don't operate that way."

"From where I sit, it looks like a good fit to me. And I'm not looking for an affair either."

She looked so beautiful and so uncertain sitting there in the moonlight, in the shadows, her heartbeat tripping at her throat, her small hands clutching her wineglass.

"What exactly are you looking for?" she asked.

It was his turn to look away. "I'm not sure," he said, knowing candor was the only answer he could offer. "The only thing I'm sure of is that you're the first woman who's ever tied me up in knots this way. You're the first woman who's made me think in terms of commitment."

He was serious and he could see that she realized it. That little truth scared her good. It scared him too. While he'd been struggling with the admission for some time, it was still as unsettling as it was appealing.

The trapped look in her eyes told him it had been much easier for her to deal with him when she'd tucked him into a safe little niche that she'd marked "short term." He'd just forced her to see him as wanting the same thing she wanted—and to know he was offering her the chance to take it.

"Tony, you're my boss."

He smiled. "That's a weak straw you're grasping, Jess. I think I've already proven that it makes no difference. No matter what happens or doesn't happen between us, your job is not a factor. Care to try again?"

"Okay. You manage to keep steering me away from it, but we need to talk about our age difference. You may be able to discount it, but it bothers me. A lot. Tony . . ." She met his eyes across the candle-light, appealing to him to listen to reason. "I'm forty-two years old."

"And I'm not," he said matter-of-factly. "When are you going to see that age makes no difference to me? Age," he insisted gently, "is a state of mind."

She closed her eyes. "That's a painfully overused cliché."

"And this is a painfully overused argument. What is it going to take to convince you that it doesn't matter? I know it's a big leap of faith to open yourself up to a relationship with me. And I know that only time is going to convince you it isn't a mistake. In the meanwhile isn't it worth the risk?

"Talk to me, Jess," he said when the silence became so unbearable, he knew there had to be more.

"I had a friend in KC," she began slowly. "She'd gone through a rough divorce. So had her next-door neighbor. He was several years younger than she, but he was hurting, too, and they began commiserating over the backyard fence."

Again looking everywhere but at him, she continued. "He was everything you are. Young. Golden. Gorgeous. The attraction was there, and she fought it because she knew it was wrong. One day he jogged over to help her with her cranky lawnmower, and the next thing she knew, they were in bed.

"He really put on the full court press then, insisting, like you, that the age difference meant nothing to him. She started to believe it, and they went straight ahead to storybook-romance time. Seeing each other every night, talking until the wee hours—even meeting each other's parents."

"Sounds terrific. So what went wrong?" he asked, knowing the other shoe was about to fall.

"What went wrong was that he lost interest. It took all of two months before she started to feel him pulling away. Then she learned the hard way that he was seeing several other women. Younger other women."

"And the conclusion you've drawn is?"

"The conclusion I've drawn is that he hadn't lied to her either. Like you he'd honestly thought the age difference didn't matter. But in the end it did."

"Would you like to hear my conclusion?" He didn't wait for her reply. "The age difference meant nothing to him because from the beginning he'd never intended to pursue a long-term relationship. And that, sweet Jess, is a very big difference from what I intend for us."

He knew she wanted to believe him. She wanted it badly. Still she fought it.

"And what if you're wrong, Tony? What if he really had wanted it to work? What if with time the same thing will happen to you that happened to him and you lose interest?" She met his eyes, revealing her doubts and fears. "I don't think I'm ready to open myself up to what she went through. It's too big a risk."

"So try another cliché on for size: Life is a risk."

She shook her head. "Not if you play it safe."

"Safe," he murmured, hanging on to his temper, determined not to let her slip away from him. "You figure if you play it safe, you won't get hurt again. The way your husband hurt you."

She didn't deny it. It still hurt her. It was written all over her face. He'd been right that night he'd brought her home in the rain. The bastard had totally destroyed her confidence in herself as a woman.

"I think we're finally getting down to what this is really all about," he said into the silence she'd left suspended between them. "And the more I think about it, the less I like it. You're not only selling me short, you're selling yourself short as well. And you know what? I like even less the idea that your ex must have done such a number on you that you can't see yourself as an attractive, sexy, totally captivating woman."

He leaned forward, making her meet his eyes. "And as much as it ticks me off that it affects me, the worst part is how much it affects you. He divorced you, you moved halfway across the country to get away from him, yet for all practical purposes he's still in your life."

Anger flared in her eyes, an anger he chose to

challenge. "He wants you back, Jess. Why don't you just go back to him?"

He'd wanted to make a point. He had. Talk about risks, he'd just taken an enormous one.

"You know I won't do that."

The hard thud of his heart told him that, no, he hadn't known. Not for certain. Relief was sweet and head clearing.

"So close the book, Jess. Don't let what he did to you determine what could happen with us."

Taking her hand in both of his, he stroked his thumb across her knuckles, all the while watching her face. "You're a very attractive woman—not just physically but as a person. You have a lot to offer a man. A lot to offer a relationship. Don't make the mistake of walking away from something that could be the best thing that ever happened to either of us just because he made you afraid to take the chance.

"I'll make you a promise, Jess," he continued when he could tell he'd gotten her attention. "When you decide you can trust what I'm telling you, when you decide you can trust what you feel, I'll make all your doubts go away the first time we make love."

It was a challenge, a gauntlet thrown.

It was also an invitation. A promise of pleasure that sent his pulse racing and heat spiraling through his blood in anticipation of fulfilling it.

But it was more than that. It was an honest appeal to her to give him a chance to prove there was more to him as a man than she was giving him credit for.

To give him a chance to show her that no obstacle was too great to come between them.

He could see that she was tempted.

"You don't play fair, Falcone."

For the first time he sensed a softening, a reluctant defeat that could ultimately mean victory for both of them.

He smiled invitingly. "I play to win."

"I'm beginning to see that."

He rose and held out his hand. "Come on. I know you need more thinking time, but I'm too wired to go home. Are you up for a little ride?"

He sensed another change in her then. A loss of that tentativeness that had compelled her to measure her every word and response with him. After a small, telling hesitation she rose and linked her hand with his, as if she'd made the decision to let him take her wherever he wanted to go. To take her into the night and trust him to keep her safe.

They drove in relative silence along Mission Boulevard, then on up the coast and eventually to La Jolla Shores.

"Where are we?" Jessie asked as he pulled over and parked along the street at the top of the ridge paralleling the beach.

"La Jolla. It's a favorite spot of mine."

He took her hand and led her down the steep steps carved into the rocky cliff that dropped almost straight down to the shoreline fifty yards below.

The early "June gloom" had broken a couple of days ago, and on this night the moon rose high and full over the Pacific. The breakers were wild and magnificent. The scent of sea permeated the air, the wind an echoing complement to the pound of salt water upon the sand.

"It's beautiful," she murmured, brushing her hair away from her face as the wind tugged and pulled and swirled around them.

He shrugged out of his jacket and settled it over her shoulders, then lifted her up and set her carefully on a flat rock. "I never get tired of coming here."

With her looking on, he removed his shoes and socks, then rolled up his pant legs.

"Hey," he said when he caught her grinning. "It's the only way to experience La Jolla.

"Come on." He helped her down. "We walk. And we talk."

Slipping the straps off her ankles, she stepped out of her sandals and took the hand he offered.

And then, against sound reason, against common sense, with her hand tucked in the warm, strong pocket of his, with the wind whipping her hair, the sand cool and wet beneath her feet, and the moon shining down as guardian and witness, she let herself fall in love.

She hadn't wanted it to happen. She hadn't wanted it to be anything more than lust. Pure, simple, basic, and biological lust. It would have been so much easier to deal with.

From the beginning, though, she'd suspected that what she was feeling for Tony was much, much more. He made her see that clearly as she listened, and learned, and gave up the fight she'd been waging.

Under the pretense of revealing more about himself, he told her things about herself she hadn't wanted to own up to. And he was right. She'd been afraid to trust her feelings. She'd let David and what he'd done to her rule her life.

The sense of self she was regaining by coming to terms with that knowledge was like a rebirth. For the first time in a long while she felt carefree and reckless and invincible. If nothing else ever came of this, she'd always thank Tony for that insight into her freedom.

Then and there she decided she was finished with hiding from her feelings because she was afraid to get them bruised again. She'd survived a beating once. If she had to, she'd survive it again.

Maybe it was foolishness on her part, but it didn't feel that way. It felt wonderful and rich and rare not to hold back any longer, to drop her guard and listen and laugh and enjoy this beautiful man at her side.

"Five brothers?" she asked, amazed, as she smiled up at him.

"And one sister."

"The poor baby."

He grinned. Moonlight danced across the stunning contours of his face as the sea breeze played with his hair.

"We spoiled her rotten. So did Mom and Dad."

"And are you all close even now?"

"Oh, yeah. All of us live within a hundred miles of here. And we all make it home for dinner once a month. You'll have to join us sometime soon."

The trepidation she had felt earlier had dimmed to a memory. The ease with which he spoke of his family made it possible. "Tell me about your mother."

His smile was as soft as the seawater rippling in the tidal pools the rocks protected. "Heart of an angel. Hand like a hammer." He chuckled. "She kept us on the straight and narrow, I'll tell you that."

"And your father?"

"Dotes on her. And on us. He made it big in real estate. Wanted to set all of us up in business."

"But you chose not to?"

He shrugged. "I tried it for a while, mostly to make him happy. It wasn't for me, though. He knew that and didn't fuss too much when I went into broadcasting."

"Just like that?"

"Not exactly. During college I played around with radio on the campus station. I liked it. The breakneck pace, the challenge. The business major was a plus."

"So you just bought a station."

"It wasn't quite that easy. After I convinced Dad that real estate wasn't for me, I managed a station for a while for Barry Lavine in Laguna Beach. He liked the job I did for him, and when KXAL came up for sale, he offered to be a silent partner if I could swing the financing."

He lifted his head to the scent of the sea. "Dad recognized a solid investment, and between the three of us we managed to cut the deal."

When she hugged his jacket around her to quell the slight chill from the damp ocean breeze, he draped an arm across her shoulders and tucked her comfortably against him.

"You're doing a good job with it."

He looked down at her, pleased. "Yes, I am. I intend to buy them both out someday. If revenues keep increasing, that day won't be all that far away."

"So," she began slowly, "that might explain something. You've been too busy moving and shaking to become involved with anyone."

He squeezed her tight and kept on walking. "Busy has nothing to do with it. What I told you earlier was the simple truth. I've never met a woman I wanted to become involved with. Until you."

He stopped and, with a hand on each of her shoulders, turned her to face him. "I want to make something clear. I haven't been a monk, Jess," he continued when she tipped her head back and met his gaze squarely. "But please believe me when I tell you, a lot of what you've heard is just talk. I'm no roving Romeo with one-nighters on my agenda and a trail of Juliets littering the path behind me."

She touched her forehead to his chest, resting there. "You're blowing your image here, Falcone."

He breathed a deep sigh. "Well, it's about damn time."

When she lifted her face to his again, he tugged a strand of wind-whipped hair from the corner of her mouth and tucked it behind her ear. "It's about damn time for this too."

Ever so slowly, his dark gaze mesmerizing and warmed by both passion and care, he lowered his mouth to hers.

Ever so slowly she lowered the last of her guard and parted her lips in invitation.

Nothing could compare to that first tentative brush of his mouth over hers. The sweet, rich anticipation. The heady hesitance born of days and nights of denial coupled with the belief that what was happening was too good to be real.

She raised a hand to his jaw, exploring what she'd wanted to touch for so long but had forced herself to deny. It was better, so much better, to let herself experience and enjoy.

He tasted of sea wind and the wine they'd shared with dinner. He tasted of promise and persuasion and of a passion long banked. His low groan made it clear he was no longer willing to deny that passion.

Jessie melted against him. Cradled in his arms, lost in the heat of his mouth, she opened to him, taking what he gave, giving back what he needed.

On a ragged breath and a tortured moan he dragged his mouth away. Tucking her head beneath his chin, he wrapped her in a crushing embrace.

"Jess. I want you," he whispered urgently. "In my

bed. Tonight. But I've got to tell you, if you keep kissing me like that, I'm going to forget my aversion to sand and we'll both have to figure out how to deal with it in the morning.

"This is not a laughing matter," he said darkly as she buried her face in his chest and gave in to a soft ripple of laughter.

"If I recall . . ." she raised her face to his, "it was *you* who picked the place to *talk*."

"Come on," he growled. Taking her hand, he tugged her with him back toward the steps.

Arms wrapped around each other, and pausing for long, silken kisses, they made their way slowly back to his car.

Jessie was the first to spot it.

"Tony . . ." She stopped in the middle of the sidewalk, all the sensuality inside her turning to disbelief, then to fear.

The windshield of his Lexus had been shattered.

"Oh, my God." Her whispered words were broken as her gaze darted frantically from his car to the swaying shadows that could be hiding whoever had done this.

Pulling her close to his side, Tony reached for the note that had been anchored beneath a wiper blade. The threatening words left no margin for belief that it had been a random act of vandalism.

"If she won't listen, maybe you will. Stay away from her."

Tony sheltered her protectively against his chest,

and she knew they were both thinking the same thing.

He could still be out there. Lurking. Stalking. Watching. Waiting for their reaction.

Beneath her cheek she could feel the angry beat of Tony's heart.

"I've got to tell you," he said tightly, "this son of a bitch is really beginning to tick me off."

EIGHT

They spent the next several hours at the La Jolla police station—frustrating hours during which Jessie's state of mind hovered somewhere between anger and despair.

Tony was protective and edgy, as disconcerted as Jessie with this unseen predator who had come too close for comfort.

The boldness of the move spoke volumes about the stalker's state of mind. If he was taking this big a chance already, it was hard telling what he'd do next. Yet the story at the La Jolla police station was the same as Tom Wayfield's.

"Until we get a bead on this guy," the officer told them, "there's nothing we can do."

He walked them to the door, his tired eyes relaying both his sympathy and the fatigue of a long day and longer years on the force. "We'll fax a copy of this report to Wayfield so he's updated. Why don't you check in with him in the morning? In the meantime we need to keep your car until the guys from Forensics can go over it tomorrow. Maybe they'll come up with something."

Jessie slumped wearily beside Tony in the backseat of the cab he'd called to take them home.

"Come 'ere," he murmured, wrapping an arm around her shoulders and drawing her snugly against his side. Then, like her, he stared in brooding silence out the window as they traveled back to her apartment. When they arrived, he paid the fare and told the cabbie not to wait.

"I'm coming in," he stated flatly when she looked at him in surprise.

Jessie could see he was in no mood to argue. "I'll make coffee."

While the coffee brewed, she leaned against the counter, drained and exhausted. Her elbows cupped in her palms, she watched Tony prowl around her apartment.

She felt the same restlessness, the inescapable edginess. And she also felt fear, but more for Tony than for herself.

This man meant to hurt Tony. If she hadn't believed that before, she did now. She was also sure that Tony wouldn't back away from the danger. If there was any hope of getting him out of the line of fire, she was the one who was going to have to do it.

How ironic, she thought. How absolutely, painfully ironic. Shaking her head, she raised her face to the ceiling. She'd finally come to terms with her feelings for him. And she was coming close to overcoming the self-doubts that could prevent her from developing a healthy relationship with a man, only to have some unknown menace threaten to end it before it ever started. It hadn't been easy convincing herself to become involved with Tony, but she'd finally decided to embrace the idea no matter what the cost.

Her cost, however, was greatly diminished when pitted against the potential cost to Tony. This person, whoever he was, whatever kind of monster he was, had made it vividly clear that he intended to hurt Tony. And for Tony's sake she saw no alternative but to back away.

She filled two mugs with coffee. Hesitant but full of purpose, she walked into the living room.

"Tony," she began when he reached for the mug she extended, "until we find this guy, I think . . . I think it would be a good idea if we made it a point not to see each other except when work absolutely requires it."

He stopped with the coffee halfway to his mouth. "I thought we'd agreed we weren't going to let this joker affect our lives."

She looked away. "Yes, well, that was before he and his friend Mr. Mallet decided to hammer the hell out of your windshield." She heard the barely veiled hysteria in her tone and drew a deep breath to calm herself.

"Tony, he means to hurt you if I don't stay away from you. For all we know, he could be out there watching us right now, getting angrier and crazier and more determined than ever. The next time it might be you he takes the hammer to." She couldn't suppress a shudder. "It's not worth the risk."

His features turned as hard as stone. "And I thought you had established that some risks were worth taking."

"They are." She pleaded with her eyes as she faced his scowl. "And the time will be right for me to take them. But we're not talking about *my* risks here, we're talking about yours. And yours involve a maniac. He wants to hurt you. That's a risk I can't, in good conscience, take."

He was silent for a long moment. "What you're suggesting is that we let him beat us."

She shook her head, refusing to accept his challenge. "No. I'm suggesting that we let him win this round. Just this round," she restated, praying he'd see the logic. "Maybe if we play it safe and keep our distance for a while, he'll lose interest."

"He's not going to lose interest, Jess," he said with chilling conviction. "You know it and I know it."

She curled up on the end of the sofa, avoiding his eyes and the accuracy of his statement. Ultimately, though, she had to admit that he was right. Bone deep she'd known it all along. Her suggestion was a pitiful grasp at a temporary solution.

Heartsick, she hugged her arms around herself and let her head fall back against the cushions. "It's like that shark in *Jaws*. Remember that movie? Everytime anyone ventured too far into deep water, the monster hovered, circled, stalked. You never knew when it was going to happen. You only knew it would. And everytime someone was fool enough to enter that water, you knew the shark was going to attack. And you knew it was going to be horrible."

He hunkered down in front of her, his large hands settling protectively on her thighs. "He's not going to attack, Jess." He met her gaze, his expression thoughtful yet decisive. "An attack would end the game for him. And I think that maybe the game is what's important to this guy. What we've got to figure out is not only why he's singled you out but who he is."

"Oh, well, I didn't realize it was that simple." Fatigue colored her frustration with sarcasm. "I've got to find a needle in a haystack tomorrow. I should have that wrapped up by noon, though, then I'll be free to pin this down. Tony, for heaven's sake, it could be one of a million guys out there!"

"Or it could be someone you know," he said carefully.

That was the second time that suggestion had been broached. She didn't like it any better now than she had the first time.

"That's ridiculous." But the thought hung there, ominous, chilling. "It's just some lunatic fan with a warped sense of reality."

"You're probably right," he said after a moment, though she sensed his acquiescence was more mollification than agreement. Rising wearily, he wandered to the window and parted the curtain. "But I don't think we should rule it out."

After a long look outside he turned back to her, his expression set, his tone determined. "In the meantime I'm tired of shadow dancing with this jerk. I think we should try to draw him out."

Her heartbeat quickened. "Draw him out?"

"Instead of seeing less of each other, I think we should start seeing more. Jess, hear me out," he said quickly when she shot off the sofa. "Instead of holding off the unveiling of the second billboard, I think I should give Brian the go-ahead to put it up right away. I want him to see it. I want him to know he doesn't have any say in what we do.

"I want to get in this guy's face," he continued, full of purpose and conviction. "I want to make him so angry that—"

"That it will drive him over the edge and he'll come after you?" she interrupted wildly.

"No." He touched a hand to her cheek to calm her. "That he'll screw up and give himself away."

Too upset to see his reasoning, she whirled away from him and fled on shaky legs to the kitchen. "Tony, I don't think . . ."

"Shhh." He was right behind her. Setting his mug on the counter, he leaned back against it, then pulled her into his arms. "Don't think. Not anymore. Not tonight. What you need is sleep. We can talk about this again in the morning. Logically. Rationally. And we'll come up with a solution, okay? Okay?" he repeated, rocking her in his arms.

She sighed in defeat. "Okay."

"Now, come on. Let's get you to bed."

She raised her gaze to his, searching, apologetic, uncertain.

He brushed the hair back from her face. "To sleep," he clarified softly. "You don't need anyone else invading your space tonight, but I'm not leaving you alone here. I'll bunk on the sofa."

She wasn't sure if it was relief or regret or equal measures of both that slogged through her body and made her sag against him.

"I'm sorry," she whispered as he walked her to her bedroom door.

"You have nothing to be sorry for. Just point me to a sheet and an extra pillow and we'll both call it a night."

With a lingering kiss he left her . . . to her empty bed and her troubled thoughts and the shadows that danced on the walls.

Was he out there? Was he watching even now?

Cocooning herself under the bedspread, she pulled a pillow over her head and hid in her own shadows, waiting for daylight to come.

Amazingly Jessie slept. Morning came as a surprise. The sunlight. The sound of the traffic on the street below. The normalcy of it. Her eyes snapped open. The fact that Tony was sleeping on her sofa.

Reality intruded far too quickly, and with it the

reminder a madman was on the prowl and she and Tony were his targets.

She rose slowly, only then realizing she'd fallen asleep fully dressed. Stiff with residual tension and a lethargy induced by a less-than-restful sleep, she stripped down to her skin. Snagging her chenille robe and slipping into it, she padded barefoot into the living room. A quick peek over the back of her sofa found Tony still sleeping.

Her heartbeat quickened dangerously at the sight he made lying there, and she reached out a hand to steady herself.

He was sprawled on his back in the cramped space, the sheet riding low and loose around his waist. Above it his arms and chest were bare. So was the large, masculine foot connected to the muscled calf that had kicked free of the lightweight sheet.

She couldn't resist a lingering look. Even in sleep he was too beautiful for words. Unguarded, relaxed, the rugged masculinity of his features mellowed into a stunning vulnerability. She had to fight to keep herself from brushing that impossibly thick, beautifully mussed black hair from his brow. The sweep of his lashes against his dark skin beckoned her to caress him, to press soft kisses to his mouth, to slowly awaken him so that she could see his eyes grow smoky and passion-filled.

With a self-censuring groan she headed for the bathroom. After shutting the door soundlessly behind her, she slipped into the shower.

They had a serious problem to deal with, she reminded herself. Making love wasn't the solution. Neither would it make their problem go away.

But the hot, steamy spray, the reality of Tony's body naked beneath the sheet that softly molded itself to his hips—naked beneath the sheet that couldn't fully hide an arousal evident even in slumber—had her trembling with both frustration and desire.

Tony's life was in danger, and all she could think of was how wonderful it would be when he made love to her. His sleekly muscled body would be solid and seductive beneath her hands. His fluid grace and wicked mouth would woo and win her moans of pleasure.

She shut off the faucets with shaking hands, buried her face in a plush towel, and willed the tremors to stop.

Her skin was still wet when she shrugged jerkily into her robe and wrapped it around her. Even with the bathroom filled with the steamy residue from the hot shower, she shivered. Not from cold but from desire. From an insatiable need that demanded and required and all but obliterated restraint and straight thinking.

Now was not the time, she told herself. This was not the place. But she felt like she was losing control, and only one thing—only one man—could ease the tension strung as tight as a guitar string. Only his loving could soothe the ache deep inside her.

She wiped the steam from the mirror with an unsteady hand. Leaning against the vanity, she closed her eyes in a bid to shut out his image, gloriously male, paganly sensual, stretched out in the other room on her sofa.

The sound of the door opening behind her stalled her heartbeat and her breath.

Slowly she forced herself to raise her gaze to the vanity mirror and meet the reflection that joined hers there.

Tony. Sleep mussed, slumberous, and wrapped in nothing but the sheet knotted low on his hips, he stood behind her in the open doorway.

Silence swelled with the promise of seduction as his eyes watched hers in the mirror. As sultry as the steam surrounding them, as intense as the pulse throbbing at the base of her throat, his look left her wanting and weak.

"Tell me to get the hell out of here," he commanded in a gruff whisper. "Tell me to leave you alone."

She swallowed, her gaze locked with his in the mirror as she watched him approach.

Watched.

And waited.

And wanted.

"Tell me I've got no business wanting you when you're this fragile . . . this uncertain . . . and this scared."

He stepped closer. So close, she could feel his heat against her back. So close, she could smell the lingering hint of his cologne, the faint kiss of the sea breeze that still clung to his hair.

She moaned and leaned into him when he hooked

his arms around her waist and pulled her back against the solid wall of his chest. His arousal nestled demandingly against her bottom.

"Tell me to stop, Jess," he said, his tone dark with passion, deep with barely leashed control as he lowered his mouth to her shoulder.

Her knees buckled.

He caught her more tightly against him.

"Jess," he whispered brokenly as his hand joined his mouth to brush her robe from her shoulder.

"Jess," he said against her neck as he trailed a path of exquisite fire across her flesh, a liquid burn that tormented and tempted and drugged her with yearning. "Stop me now . . ."

His murmur was as ragged and as rough as the warm, calloused hand that had teamed with his mouth to seduce her. With a dazed longing she watched in the mirror, anticipating each move as he dragged her robe aside and finally possessed her breast with his hand.

Gripping the lip of the vanity on either side of her hips, she cried out in pleasure, in surrender, in a reckless joy that praised and pleaded and told him everything but "Stop."

His mouth moved like velvet against her skin; his hand stroked and massaged and sent her heart into a wild, thundering storm of elation.

She reached back and sank her fingers into his thick hair as he bent his head to her neck. The erotic picture they made in the mirror was as arresting as his touch. His dark hair was satin and seduction. Her own hair fell in her eyes, caught in her mouth.

Falling open, her robe slipped completely off her shoulders, exposing both breasts, heavy with arousal, her nipples tight and erect.

He raised his head, his eyes lambent with desire as he banded his arm tighter around her. He watched with her as his nimble fingers and broad palm caressed and finessed and drew from her a low, needy moan.

The contrasts were erotically stunning. His steely strength, her soft femininity. The deep tan of his skin, the milky whiteness of hers.

"Tony," she gasped as he rolled her nipple between his forefinger and thumb, ground his hips against her bottom.

With a ragged oath he spun her around, pinning her between himself and the vanity. She sagged back against the mirror, her breath coming in short, choppy pants as he bent his head to her breast to sip and nip and strip her of speech and restraint. She'd become a creature of feeling, of sensations too delicious to savor slowly, too impossibly demanding to deny.

Knotting her fingers in his hair, she arched her back, pressing her shoulders into the cold mirror and her breast into the hot, wet velvet of his mouth.

The sounds he made were lusty and lush, his touch greedy and giving as he bracketed her ribs with his hands and pulled her closer still. His lips tugged and suckled, and need shot from her breast to her belly. It pooled and heated there, then spread like melting honey to pulse and swell in an aching heat between her thighs.

With a long, lingering caress of his mouth, he raised his head and looked at her. What she saw in his eyes was more beautiful than any promise her ex-husband had ever made and then broken. Dusky heat and a smoldering desire. Silent need and a demanding passion.

Lord help her, he was beautiful. Gloriously wild, magnificently aroused. The silver falcon around his neck caught the light and gave the illusion of flight, soaring as her heart soared under his smoky gaze.

She touched his face. He closed his eyes, drew in a rough breath, then opened them again to search her face with a seeking intensity.

His gaze locked on hers, he lifted her onto the vanity, parted her thighs, and moved between them. She wrapped her legs around his hips as he reached for the belt at her waist and tugged it free. The robe pooled around her, baring her completely.

"I knew you'd be like this," he whispered, watching his hand as he placed it on her pale belly.

She sucked in a sharp breath as he spread his fingers wide and in a slow, massaging glide, slid his hand up her body.

She followed his gaze to where the heel of his palm pressed possessively against her breastbone. More delicious contrasts, she mused. Slim fingers spread wide between plump white breasts. The rapid thrum of her heartbeat under the hot caress of his eyes.

"I want you so badly," he whispered, his voice husky and edging toward wildness.

A cry caught in her throat when he bent to taste her belly with his tongue. Fire, fluid and searing, arced from the spot his mouth caressed to her most intimate, most needy places.

"Stop me now, Jess," he murmured, seducing with his lips and tongue and the brush of his hair across her quivering flesh. "If you don't want this, stop me now before it's too late."

Too late. Too late. Two words. Too true. Impossible to deny.

"It's already too late," she murmured, embracing the inevitable, anticipating the glorious end. Too late to turn back. Too late to deny the golden pleasure he promised.

She'd been hurting for too long, doubting herself as a woman for too long. And in the midst of the madness the stalker created, she needed a haven. She needed Tony and the pride he could return to her, the sweet love he could make that offered the promise of oblivion.

"Too late," she whispered again, a surrender, a plea. An offering. "It was too late the first time I saw you."

She reached for him, shifting her weight to get closer as he slid up her body.

Cradling her hips in his big hands, he pulled her against him and took her mouth in a carnal, consuming kiss. Whatever hesitancy might have been lurking in her subconscious dissipated like mist at dawn as he dragged her deeper into their passion.

He possessed her with his strength, wooed her with his gentleness, and won her with the sweeping, intimate invasion of his tongue.

His mouth took control, seeking and demanding. He conquered with bruising kisses, coaxed with healing tongue strokes, then pulled away only long enough to rid himself of the sheet.

He groaned as he brushed himself against her. The coarse silk of his chest hair abrading her sensitized nipples added another sensation, another swift and thrilling rush of sensual heat and sexual healing.

She didn't remember it ever being like this, this feeling of strength and fragility that eddied through her blood and left her reeling and weak. And wanting more. More of Tony and the feelings he introduced, then dared her to deny. She didn't want to deny anything. She wanted to feel, and share, and stretch each facet of this rebirth to the limit.

With Tony, though, she was learning there were no limits. With Tony there were no inhibitions. When he gathered her against him and, with her legs locked around his waist, walked her into the hallway, she gladly went along for the ride.

When he lay her gently on the carpeted floor and told her to forget about boundaries, she obeyed him.

When he rolled to his back and with his eyes told her where he wanted her, she straddled him without hesitation.

And when he reached for her and drew her to him, she assumed the dominant role he'd intuitively sensed she needed.

Teasing him with the elusive glide of her breasts across his chest, tempting him with the seductive brush of her nipples against his lips, she swayed above him. Temptress. Lover. Woman coming to terms with the power of her sexuality.

She met his eyes and saw his approval . . . and his excitement as she lowered her mouth to his and kissed him the way he'd just taught her he liked to be kissed. Open-mouthed. Wet and hungry.

He groaned and, locking his arms around her, rolled her to her back beneath him. Never taking his mouth from hers, he skimmed his hand along her belly, hesitating only to press the heel of his palm against her mound as a prelude to the penetration of his finger.

Capturing her moan in his mouth, he thrust his tongue slowly, suggestively, in and out of the depths of her mouth, mirroring the action with the glide of his finger in and out of her body.

She was wet and hot and swollen with need. And just that fast she came. With a breathy cry she climaxed. Shocked, shattered, convulsing around his finger, she cried his name and hung on as he took her for the ride of her life.

Her heartbeat hadn't yet slowed, her head hadn't stopped reeling, when his beautiful weight was over her again. Nudging her legs apart with his knee, he fit himself inside her. And the sensations began again.

He was sleek velvet strength, granite hard and consuming. And he filled not only her body but the void of a year too long without love.

Love. The word was a haunting reality tangled with the knowledge that sex was not the true issue here.

Love. She'd tried to deny it since the moment she'd set eyes on him. Not anymore.

Love had everything to do with this. She'd never given herself the way she was giving to Tony. Only love could motivate her to trust and share and expose herself so completely.

Only love could have her clinging and crying his name as he plunged inside her, and in one final, golden stroke, rocketed them into the silken abyss together.

When he could manage it, Tony levered himself up on his elbows and looked down at the woman lying limp and sated beneath him.

Shaken by the depths of his passion, thrilled by the openness of hers, he knew he'd found something rare. What they'd just shared was indescribable.

And she . . . she was incredible. Everything he'd hoped for, more than he'd dreamed. She'd taken him to paradise and beyond with her honest responses and lack of inhibition. Nothing, and no one, was ever going to take her away from him.

Lowering his head again, he nuzzled the silken skin of her jaw, nipping, caressing, his desire reawakening as she stirred and stretched languidly beneath him.

"You survived, then," he whispered, smiling down at her. "You were so quiet, I was beginning to wonder."

Ever so slowly she opened her eyes. They were hazy with latent passion.

"I survived," she assured him, her own smile lazy and content as she stretched again. Threading her fingers through his hair, she brushed it back from his face. "But rest assured, if I hadn't, I'd have died a deliriously happy woman."

He chuckled and kissed her inner arm. "And you're not sorry." Even he heard the tension in his voice, the concern that in the aftermath she'd realize he'd seduced her and would resent him for taking away her choice.

She blinked, moisture glistening in her eyes and, if possible, making them even more lustrous.

"How could I be sorry for one of the most beautiful experiences of my life?"

He swallowed back the sudden thickening in his throat as she touched his lips. With a low groan he captured her fingers with his teeth and sucked them inside his mouth.

Her sigh caught on a breathless hitch.

"Do you have any idea what it does to me when you look at me like that?"

Her laugh was husky and low and as erotic as the lingering scent of their lovemaking. She arched her hips provocatively against him. "I think I have a pretty good idea."

"Speaking of good ideas . . ." He braced himself, stiff-armed, above her. "I know there's a bed in this apartment. I think it would be an excellent idea if we made use of it."

"I like the way you think."

"And I like the way you look," he murmured as he picked her up. He carried her to her bed and laid her across pastel sheets that smelled of her.

Lowering his head to her breast, he nipped and licked and nuzzled a berry-red and prettily pouting nipple. "And the way you taste."

He pulled his mouth away, his muscles trembling with the need to take her again. "And the way you feel when I'm inside you."

Watching her face, he touched her again, intimately. "Jess . . . you're so hot."

She bit her lower lip and moaned. "Tony, stop. I . . . I can't hold—"

"I don't want you to," he whispered, stroking, teasing, playing his fingers along her feminine flesh as she arched against his hand. "Don't hold back. I want you to come apart for me. And I want to see your face when it happens. Go with it, Jess," he murmured, coaxing her higher. "Let yourself fly."

With a throaty cry she not only flew, she soared for him. It was the most beautiful sight he'd ever witnessed. At least it was until he lowered his body over hers and watched her eyes glaze at the strength of his possession.

He loved her slowly this time. Without urgency. Without haste. With deep, languid strokes and long, lazy kisses that led them sweetly to an end as satisfying as the reality of finally making her his.

When it was over and she was clinging and weeping softly in his arms, he held her with a sense of reverence that was as empowering as it was humbling.

So this was love.

He'd always wondered what all the fuss was about. Wondered what it was that made a man weak with longing, strong with purpose. What he'd been missing.

Jessie. Jessie was what he'd been missing.

His chest was full of feelings too rich to catalog, too rare to equate to experience. So he simply held her, stroking the damp hair back from her temples, murmuring his praise, whispering his promises. Thanking the powers that be that she'd come into his life.

Finally she slept. With great reluctance he left her bed and headed for the shower.

Whistling softly, he emerged from the steamy warmth of the bathroom, drying his hair with a towel and thinking about making love with her again.

He stopped dead in his tracks, his heart slamming against his chest, when he saw her standing by her desk.

The phone hung limply from her hand.

Her eyes were wild with terror.

NINE

Flinging the towel aside, Tony rushed over to her. "What?" he demanded, afraid he already knew the answer.

She cradled the receiver with a trembling hand. "It—it was him."

He didn't have to ask who she meant. He didn't have to wonder at the new dimension of fear clouding her eyes. The bastard had not only found out where she lived, somehow he'd managed to get hold of her unlisted phone number.

One look at her pale face, and he knew that she understood the significance and the implication. The phone call let her know in no uncertain terms that he could reach them anytime he wanted to.

"What did he say?"

She shook her head and looked away.

His rage that she was frighteningly vulnerable

spilled over as he gripped her by both arms. "Dammit, Jess, tell me what he said."

She gathered herself and forced the words out. "He . . . he said that what I'd done was unforgivable. He said I never should have let you in my bed. And . . . and he said he'd make us both sorry."

He drew her roughly to him.

"He's watching us."

Her muffled whisper tore at him. He sank his fingers into her hair and held her closer.

"All the time he's watching us. How did he know?" She shoved herself out of his arms, raking the hair back from her face. *"How did he know?"*

"He doesn't know," he said, trying to interject some sense of calm. "He's just guessing."

"Damn good guess, wouldn't you say?"

"He only wants to scare you."

"Well, guess what?" She laughed, a harsh, wounded sound that held no humor. "He's doing a fine job of that too."

"Jess . . ." She tried to spin away from him, but his hand on her arm stopped her. "Jess, listen to me. He'll use your fear to control you. Are you going to let him do that?"

"What choice do I have?"

"We always have choices. Listen to me," he said again, holding her firmly when she tried to jerk away. "I'm going to ask you to make a choice right now. I'm going to ask you to trust me. To know what to do. To protect you."

He watched her carefully, gauging her control.

"Can you do that? Can you make the choice to put your life in my hands?"

Her eyes hardened with purpose. "Not if it means it will place you in danger."

Gentling his tone and his hold, he touched a hand to her cheek. "You let me worry about me."

She looked so small yet so full of determination as she clung to the notion of somehow protecting him by sacrificing herself.

"Trust, Jess. That's what it's all going to boil down to. Complete trust. I need you to trust me."

"I do," she whispered. "I do trust you."

"Then pack a bag. You're moving out of here."

She looked up sharply at him.

"And moving in with me."

A long silence passed before she nodded. He squeezed her shoulders in encouragement and breathed a sigh of relief.

Tony knew he had railroaded Jessie into moving in with him. He wasn't proud of it, but he really didn't care. The important thing was that she was going to be with him. If that jerk decided to come after her, at least Tony had the satisfaction of knowing the stalker would have to get past him first.

"Did you get things squared with Sarah?" he asked as she hung up her phone.

"I think so." She offered him a tight, controlled smile. While she still looked shaken, she'd pulled herself together admirably. "I told her there had been a major plumbing problem with the apartment building. She thinks I'm moving into a motel for a few days until it's repaired. I asked her to call the station if she needs to reach me, since she thinks I don't yet know where I'll be staying."

"It was hard lying to her," he concluded.

"Yes, but it would be harder telling her what's been happening. I want to keep her in the dark for as long as possible. She has enough to deal with at school without worrying about me. Fortunately she's flying home tomorrow for the break before summer classes start. Counting the long Memorial Day weekend, she'll be in Kansas City for nine days."

"With a little luck we'll have this over by then."

"One way or another," she added, that trapped look returning to her eyes.

"Jess, you said you'd trust me, right? Then believe this. Nothing is going to happen to you—or to me. Come on. We'll drop off your things at my place, make a trip over to talk with Tom Wayfield again, and then we'll head for the station. We've got a show to do tonight and a plan to set in motion."

And hopefully, he added silently as they locked her apartment door behind them, by the time they reached the station he'd figure out what that plan was.

Someone else had been making plans too. When they finally reached the station around five P.M., Tony wasn't at all pleased with the turn of events.

"I'm sorry, honey," Clarice said, sounding frazzled and more than apologetic when she told Jessie that her ex-husband was waiting in her office to see her.

"I didn't know what to do," Clarice went on. "When he said he was your husband and that he needed to see you, I thought maybe it might have something to do with Sarah."

"It's okay, Clarice. You did the right thing. It probably is about Sarah—"

"Jess," Tony cut in, "I need to talk to you for a minute first."

Without waiting for her reply, he grabbed her by the hand. Leading her past an obviously interested Brian and a couple of staring salesmen, he tugged her into his office.

"Husband?" he grumbled when he'd closed the door behind them. "He's got a lot of nerve, I'll give him that."

"I'm sure she misunderstood him."

"Right," he muttered. Realizing how proprietary he was acting, he backed off. He studied her face, but her feelings were guarded behind a stoic frown. Gaining new appreciation for the force of the green-eyed monster, he wished he could guard his as well.

"Do you want me to make myself scarce?" he asked finally, considering the offer a major concession on his part.

"I think that would probably be best. Tony . . ." She touched his arm. "David is Sarah's father. We're going to have to have contact from time to time. It's unavoidable."

"That doesn't mean I have to like it."

She searched his face, her eyes troubled. "No, it doesn't. But it's part of what I bring with me. If you can't deal with it—"

"I can deal with it," he said, cutting her off. Running a hand through his hair, he cursed his stupidity and settled himself down. "I'm sorry. I know I'm not handling this well. Jealousy is a new emotion for me."

She smiled. "You have nothing to be jealous of."

"Yeah, well, from where I sit, I see it a little differently." Taking her hands in his, he eased a hip onto his desk and drew her toward him. "The man wants you back, Jess. He was a big part of your life for a long time. He knows things about you that I may never know."

He looked down at their joined hands. "You made love with him," he said after a long pause. "You made a child with him." Insecurity, Tony mused. Another new emotion. Completely foreign, totally defeating. He wrestled to get it under control, taking small solace in the excuse that he was worried about her.

"You're the man in my life now, Tony." Her voice was soft with understanding. "It wasn't a decision I made lightly, and it's not one I'm going to back away from."

He let out a deep breath, then offered the only explanation he could. "You mean so much to me, Jess."

She squeezed his hands. "I know."

Squaring his shoulders, he met her gaze. "I guess you'd better go see what he wants."

"Do you want to meet him?"

With that offer she told him she not only understood his feelings but that she forgave him for his foolishness.

He grinned sheepishly. "One way or the other I was going to make damn sure I did."

She laughed and tugged him toward the door. "Come on, then. I'd just as soon orchestrate the introduction as worry about your surprise entrance."

As they walked into her office, Jessie tried to see David through Tony's eyes. Given the history they shared, she thought it would be difficult to distance herself for an objective look. It wasn't.

At forty-five David was still an attractive man. Elegantly slim, impeccably dressed in a gray pinstripe Brooks Brothers suit and blue shirt a few shades lighter than his eyes, he emanated exactly what he was—successful, self-possessed, and to some, she supposed, an intimidating man.

If she'd occasionally questioned the possibility of lingering feelings for him, seeing him again gave her a definitive answer. The only emotion she felt was regret for what the breakup of their marriage had done to Sarah.

She had to give Tony credit. After a quick handshake and a promise to see her later, he left, closing the door behind him.

"I didn't know you were coming out to fly back to Kansas City with Sarah." She motioned for David to take a chair as she rounded her desk and sat down.

He smiled the smile that had charmed her all those years ago. No doubt it still had the same devastating effect on some women that it had once had on her.

"It was a last-minute decision," he said easily. "The truth is I wanted a chance to see you. How are you doing, Jessie?" he added in an intimate tone when she remained silent.

She leaned forward, folding her hands on the top of her desk. "I'm fine. And I can see you're well too. But I'm sure you're not here to check on my health or my state of mind. What's this visit really about?"

He looked momentarily surprised before another smile touched his mouth. "You've changed. The Jessie I was married to would have made small talk before confronting an issue head-on."

"Well, I guess that perception might explain a few things. I haven't changed, David. I'm the same woman I was a year ago."

The look in his eyes told her that he hadn't missed her implication.

"Would it make a difference to you, then," he asked, "if I told you that *I* was a different man? I made a mistake, Jessie," he added after a meaningful pause.

She'd been afraid that was what this visit was

about. Yet as much as she'd dreaded it, now that he'd broached the subject, she was glad for the opportunity to put the confrontation behind them.

"That may very well be true. But it's done, and there's no going back."

He studied the floor between his feet before meeting her eyes again. "I'm sorry, Jessie. Really sorry that it was so difficult for you."

"Sarah's the one who suffered." Hearing the brittleness in her tone, she threw more effort into curbing her resentment. "And as long as we're discussing Sarah, please don't make it harder on her by intimating that there's a chance we could get back together."

His blue eyes softened with appeal. "Is that really such a bad idea?"

His appeal, however, triggered irritation instead of empathy. Again for Sarah's sake, she willed herself not to show it. "It's not only a bad idea, David, it's not even a remotely viable one."

Her response obviously surprised him. And then it angered him. "Because of Falcone?" His tone was biting and accusatory. "I saw the way you looked at him."

"What I do and the choices I make," she said slowly and distinctly, "no longer concern you."

One corner of his mouth quirked up sardonically. "Never figured you'd fall for a set of shoulders and a macho line."

And she'd never figured he'd leave her. But she didn't say it. It was no longer a point of contention.

Neither was she willing to discuss her relationship with Tony.

"I don't want to trade insults with you, David. And as far as I can see, this conversation is serving no purpose. Before we both say something we'll regret, maybe you'd better leave."

He leaned forward, elbows propped on his thighs, his expression intent and judgmental. "Jessie, stop. Think of Sarah."

"Me?" she cried incredulously, giving in to the outrage stirred up by his unjust remark. "You're asking me to think of Sarah when you're the one who left us? When you're the one who's using her to get to me, now that you want to piece back together what *you* tore apart?" She shook her head. "Don't insult me or yourself by even suggesting that I have a reason to feel responsible."

He stared at her long and hard, his own anger and defensiveness evident in the tense set of his shoulders and the rigid jut of his jaw.

"So you think your young Italian stud is your answer. Well, I hate to tell you, but you're only succeeding in making a fool of yourself."

His accusation stung more than it should have. A small part of her was still afraid that what he'd said was true. Hating herself for letting him get to her, she shifted uncomfortably in her chair. "And you're only succeeding in making me angry. Please leave."

He stood slowly, strode to the door, but stopped when he reached it. "You're making a mistake, Jessie."

You're making a mistake, Jessie.

She froze as his words, the exact words the caller had used, echoed with haunting clarity. Rising stiffly, she struggled to shrug off the unsettling coincidence and the flash of fear his statement triggered.

"No, David," she said, regaining her composure. "It's like you said—you're the one who made the mistake. I'd suggest you learn to live with it.

"And David . . ." She met his gaze when he turned back to her. "I bowed out of your life gracefully a year ago when you asked me to. It's only fair that you return the favor."

After a long, silent moment he walked out.

The door had barely closed behind him when she heard a soft rap.

Without waiting for an invitation, Tony stepped inside. Watching her face, he leaned back against the door and crossed his arms over his chest.

"Stockbroker?" he asked conversationally.

She drew a deep breath, her anger slowly abating. "Sales rep," she said, sinking down in her chair.

"Snake oil?" he ventured with a nasty smile as he walked toward her.

His irreverent sense of humor diminished the sting of David's barbs. She grinned. "Pharmaceuticals."

He shrugged. "Same thing."

That brought a genuine laugh. "He regards you highly too."

"Yeah?" He tugged her to her feet, then dropped

down in her chair and resituated her on his lap. "Impressed with my business savvy, was he?"

She toyed with the falcon shimmering at his throat, her smile coy, her eyes teasing as they both relaxed, confident again in their feelings for each other. "Actually your heritage, your broad shoulders, your youth, and your obvious machismo made more of an impression. Oh—and I distinctly recall the word *stud* coming up."

He snorted. "The man's more perceptive than he looks."

"Accurate too," she added, playing along.

"I've always wanted to be a sex object."

"Well, if this morning was any indication, Mr. Falcone, your potential will be exceeded only by—"

"My staying power," he finished huskily, drawing her against him. "And my creativity. Did I tell you what I have in mind for tonight?"

She groaned. "No. And if you want me to get through the broadcast, you'd be wise to keep your plans to yourself."

"You're the only thing I want to keep to myself." His eyes turned serious again. "Have we seen the last of him?"

She considered for a moment before nodding. "I think so."

"Good. Because I've got to tell you, I didn't like the guy."

"I think we can safely say the feeling was mutual."

He ignored her sarcasm. "I mean it, Jess. Something about him really bothered me."

"Let's do an objectivity check here, Falcone."

The hands linked across her lap clenched tighter. "No, it's not just because you were married to him. It's something else. I can't pinpoint it."

"And *I* don't want to talk about him anymore, okay?"

He read the warning on her face and hugged her hard. "You're right. Enough about him. How are you feeling about other things? You doing okay?"

The other things he was referring to had to do with his and Tom's plan of attack against the stalker. While she was still reluctant because of the element of danger it held for Tony, she had agreed to go along with the plan.

She eased off his lap and walked over to the small window. "Yes, I'm okay."

She just wanted it over. Even as they spoke, she clung to that thought, knowing that steps were already being taken.

Under Tom's direction her home phone, Tony's phone, and the station lines were being tapped with the San Diego police department's most sophisticated electronic surveillance devices. Further, as long as Tom could afford the manpower, every move they made from this point on would be monitored. He'd even enlisted the assistance of the El Cajon police to have a cruiser stationed within minutes of Tony's house. In addition undercover detectives would shadow the Falcon and the Fox's public appearance at a promotion for a new nightclub the following night.

She turned back to him, pushing away her worry over the vulnerability inherent in such an encounter with the public. "I'm so glad Sarah is going to be away from this."

"Do you want me to drive you over to see her before she leaves tomorrow?"

"I don't think so. I'll call her in a little bit and say my good-byes. I'm afraid if I see her in person, I'll give something away. She's very perceptive. About many things."

"Many things . . . as in us? You think she'll be okay with it?"

Jessie shrugged. "Time will tell. But I have confidence she's adult enough to handle it."

"She's strong, like her mother."

"I don't feel very strong right now." Hugging her arms around her waist, she shivered. "And I don't like myself much because of it."

"Hey." He went to her, drawing her into his arms. "You're doing fine. And you have reason to be a little rattled. But it's going to be over soon. Maybe even after tomorrow night."

Tomorrow night. She had a bad feeling about tomorrow night. She snuggled against him and prayed that he was right. "Is that a promise, Mr. Falcone?" she asked, forcing a lightness she didn't even come close to feeling.

"The first of many."

❧————————————————❧

Later that night, wrapped in the warmth of Tony's arms, sated and spent from the wonders of his lovemaking, it was easy for Jessie to believe in the promises he made.

He'd promised her ecstasy; he'd given her more. With every touch, every kiss, with whispered words and the golden strokes of his body, he'd fulfilled that promise far beyond her wildest dreams.

"I never knew," she murmured, caressing the dark head that lay across her breast. "I never knew it could be like this."

He wrapped his arms tighter around her. His warm breath whispered across her skin, making her shiver.

"And I've always known." Raising his head, he braced himself above her on his elbows, cocooning her in the strong haven of his arms. "I've always known that something was missing with other women. What I didn't know was that it was something this special.

"What I didn't know, Jess," he repeated, brushing feathery kisses to her brow, "was that I had feelings like this inside me."

Humbled by the depth of his emotion, she touched a hand to his jaw, then lovingly cradled his cheek in her palm.

"I want you with me, Jess. When this is over, I want you to stay."

Silence, as significant as his statement, filled the

room, crowding into the cozy bed, along with her doubts.

"Those are mighty big words, partner." The quaver in her voice negated her attempt at sounding playful and light. "I'd understand if, come sunrise, you want to take them back."

"Take them back?" His smile warmed her in places that had been cold for a long time. "I'm taking nothing back. And I'm just getting started.

"Jess . . ." He paused, sobering abruptly. "I know that with this threat hanging over our heads, my timing stinks, but there's something I need to say to you."

Only moonglow diluted the darkness of his bedroom. Still, she could see the intensity on his face. And she understood the importance of what he was about to tell her.

"I love you, Jess. Irrevocably. Completely. With everything that's in me, with everything I have to give.

"And I know this probably sounds clichéd," he whispered, as with gentle fingers he brushed away the tears she'd given up trying to hold back, "but that's something I've never said to a woman. It's something I thought I'd never say. Because I never intended to say it unless I meant it.

"I love you, Jess," he repeated, punctuating each word with the caress of his lips on hers. "Only you. Always you.

"You don't have to say anything. I just needed you to know it. And to know that whatever it takes to make you love me, consider it done. I'd scale mountains for you, Jess. I'd walk through fire."

She watched his face through a blur of tears, too filled with emotion to speak. His eyes were glistening, too, with the love he professed and, she suspected, with uncertainty about her feelings for him.

She moved beneath him, pulled him to her, wrapped her arms around him, and held on as if she'd never let go.

"You are an incredible man, Tony Falcone," she murmured. "And right or wrong, foolish or wise, I love you too. If I'd ever had any doubt, what we've shared in each other's arms erased it. And if I'm foolish for believing we can actually have a future together, then I'd rather be a fool than spend another day without you."

Cupping his face in her hands, she brought his mouth to hers for a deep, silken kiss. A kiss of promise. Of forever. Of trust and understanding that opened a world of possibilities between them.

"Believe it," he said, breaking the kiss. "And believe this. Everything, *everything*, is going to be perfect."

The next morning started out that way. Perfect.

Jessie was perfectly lazy and perfectly content as she snuggled deeper into Tony's bed. The bed that smelled of him and of the lingering, lusty scent of their lovemaking.

Without opening her eyes she rolled onto her

stomach toward the center of the mattress. Flinging her arm in the general direction of his pillow, she searched for the warmth of his body, the silk of his hair . . . and connected with a huge pile of fur instead.

Her eyes shot open. She jerked her hand back and reared up on her elbows.

Tut was curled up on Tony's pillow, his cool topaz eyes staring a hole through the center of her forehead.

"I see you two are getting acquainted."

She rolled over on her back to find Tony standing in the doorway, a breakfast tray in his hands, a bath towel knotted at his hips.

"I guess you could call it that." Dragging the hair out of her eyes, she scooted up in bed, tugging the covers with her. She propped a pillow behind her and leaned back against the headboard. "We may have a problem here. I don't think your cat likes me."

"*I* like you." One corner of his mouth tilted up suggestively as he walked to the bed.

She grinned. "Well good. Because if push came to shove, I'd pick you over the cat any day. He definitely has an attitude."

"You just have to learn how to read him."

She turned back to Tut. The same stark, regal gaze stared back at her with feline superiority. "Dislike," she decided, returning Tut's stare. "I definitely read dislike."

Tony chuckled. "He's just a little proprietary. He's not used to sharing the house with anyone but me. Once he knows you're here to stay, he'll make nice."

It didn't take much effort to curb a semiobligatory urge to reach out and pet the cat. "And how does one know when Tut is making nice?"

"He'll share his mice with you."

"Yuck. Tony!"

"I'm teasing." Laughing at her sour face, he set the tray on the bedside table and sat down beside her. "Speaking of nice, I can't think of anything nicer than waking up and finding you in my bed."

"I think I could get used to it too," she said, reaching for him. "And to this . . ."

She pulled him into a long, slow kiss.

"How are you?" he asked, licking the taste of her from his lips as she leaned back against the pillows again.

"I am wonderful."

"There, you see? You and Tut already have something in common. He purrs like that, too, when he's content. Only it takes more than a scratch behind the ears and a saucer of milk to get that sound out of you."

"Not much more," she said, reddening when she thought of the way he'd made love to her in the middle of the night. "And definitely not much more this morning. Food will do the trick. I'm starving."

"I might just be able to do something about that."

"Yeah?" She sliced a glance toward the covered tray. "Well, I'll warn you right now, if the only thing under that napkin is a saucer of milk, that cat's in for a fight . . . or did you bring me something better?"

"You mean better than me?"

"Nothing's better than you. Before that gleam in your eyes gets too bright, though, I've got to tell you . . . if I don't get nourishment soon, I won't be capable of feeding myself, let alone doing what I think you have in mind."

His grin turned positively wicked. "If you could read that cat's mind as well as you can read mine, you two won't have a problem."

It was her turn to grin. "Mind reading has little to do with it."

He cocked his head. "No?"

"No. It was the towel that gave you away."

He looked down at his lap. "Oh." Then back at her, his eyes glittering. "I see what you mean."

She laughed. "I think I'm in trouble. And whether you want to admit it or not, this age difference may give us more problems than either one of us had thought. I don't know if I can keep up with you."

"Well, I'll tell you, little Fox . . ." He leaned close, his voice suggestive and low as he nuzzled at the sheet she'd hugged to her breasts. "You get too tired, you let me know, okay? I'll see to it that you get plenty of bedrest."

"Tony . . . I . . . ah . . ." She sucked in a tortured breath when he found her nipple beneath the sheet and started sucking. "I . . . I really need . . . breakfast."

He pulled away. "Then by all means, let's have breakfast."

She watched with suspicion as he whipped the napkin off the tray.

"The strawberries and whipped cream are for you." His eyes met hers with a dark, daring invitation. "The chocolate sauce is for me."

She swallowed hard. "Chocolate sauce? For breakfast?"

His grin was unrepentant and wonderfully telling as he dipped a beautiful ripe berry into the whipped cream.

"You have breakfast your way," he murmured, tucking the berry into her mouth. After ridding himself of his towel and tugging her sheet free, he reached for the chocolate sauce. "I'll have it mine."

Watching his face, she bit into the sweet, juicy fruit with a low, delicious moan, then shivered in anticipation as he drizzled the warm chocolate sauce over the tip of one breast, then the other. Her stomach muscles convulsed when he trickled a thick stream of chocolate down the center of her body.

She sank back against the pillows with a breathless shiver. "Tony . . ."

"Shhh." He bent his head to her breast and slowly followed the trail of chocolate with his mouth, licking, tasting, feasting.

"When I get through with you," he whispered, nipping the sensitive flesh on the inside of her thigh, "you'll never think of breakfast in bed in quite the same way again."

TEN

It was noon before Jessie had recovered enough to make her way out of bed and into the shower.

Wrapped in her robe, she followed the scent of freshly brewed coffee to the kitchen. After pouring herself a cup, she wandered around the house, finally spotting Tony outside on the patio scribbling in a notebook.

His smile was mellow and content when she joined him.

"Good morning. Again," he added, then chuckled when her face gave away that she was thinking about the first time she'd awakened that morning and the exquisite but shocking way he'd enjoyed his . . . chocolate.

"I hope you never stop doing that."

"Doing what?"

"Blushing."

She sat down in the chair beside him. "Something tells me you'll continue to find ways to ensure I won't be able to stop."

"We aim to please."

It was her turn to chuckle. "If your aim was any better, I don't think I'd survive it."

"Which is why I made you breakfast. A *real* breakfast this time."

He lifted the lid from a thermal tray filled with scrambled eggs and toast. "There're more berries in the bowl. And some melon."

"And he cooks too." She sighed with theatrical ecstasy. "Your mother raised you right."

After filling her plate, she sat back to enjoy the beauty of the warm California day. The sun was shining brightly, a breeze sang sweetly through the hills. At the farthest corner of Tony's manicured lawn, a mother quail and her young skittered merrily back and forth, pecking the ground for their morning meal.

"It's beautiful up here."

"I've always thought so. I'm glad you think so too."

"I do. And it shows me another side of you." Her gaze traveled to the roses so lovingly tended and the bird feeders brimming with feed. "You're a very special man."

"I love a woman who knows a good thing when she sees it."

He leaned across the table to plop a huge, smacking kiss on her cheek before going back to his scribbling.

"What are you doing?" she asked when she'd satisfied the better part of her appetite.

His pen stilled on the paper. "You won't like the answer."

She paused, a forkful of eggs poised in mid-air.

"I'm making a list of potential suspects."

Her appetite suddenly gone, she set the fork down and sat back in her chair. "Oh."

"Yeah, oh. You won't like this either. Your ex is at the top of the list."

"David?" She pushed her plate away. "I know you don't like him, but to suspect him is ridiculous."

"Is it?"

"For heaven's sake, Tony—"

"Think about it, Jess," he cut in. "He wants you back. He might be desperate enough to try anything to accomplish it."

Resistant to the idea, but thoughtful, she replayed David's visit yesterday. *You're making a mistake.* Those had been his exact words just before he'd left her office. The same words the caller had used. She shook her head. While disturbing, it was a coincidence. It had to be.

"Tony, please," she argued, refusing to accept what he was suggesting. "David lives in KC. He couldn't possibly have done any of those things."

"He travels a lot, doesn't he? It might interest you to know that he's made several trips to San Diego during the past month."

Her brow furrowed, but then she shook her head.

"No. I'd have known if he'd been here. Sarah would have told me."

"Unless Sarah didn't know." He paused meaningfully, then added, "Tom checked it out."

"Tom Wayfield's been checking on David?"

He nodded. "He was here, Jess."

That set her back for a moment. "Then he was here on business."

He conceded with a small shrug. "Could be. But like I said, until we get this pinned down, everyone is a suspect." After a long pause he leveled her again. "Who is Steven?"

Her gaze shot to his. "Steven? How do you know about Steven?"

Looking uncomfortable, avoiding her eyes, he bounced the tip of his pen up and down on his notepad. "Tom called this morning. Their electronic surveillance picked up a call from him on your answering machine last night."

"Steven is not a suspect, Tony," she said adamantly. "He's a friend. A very good friend."

Tony wanted more, she could see it in his eyes. She couldn't bring herself to give it, though. Somehow it seemed like a betrayal of Steven's friendship.

"If he's a friend, then I'm sure he's okay," Tony said after a tense minute. "But just to be safe, Tom wants his full name and address. He'll never know he's being investigated, okay?"

She rose quickly from the table. Dragging a hand through her hair, she walked to the corner of the patio, leaning against a wrought-iron pillar to steady herself.

The day that had begun so perfectly had turned as sour as spoiled milk. She no longer saw the beauty. And instead of birdsong she heard nothing but the recurrent drone of anxiety that had invaded her life since the calls had begun.

"This is all so awful."

"I know. I'm sorry, Jess," Tony said from behind her.

Drawing a fortifying breath, she turned back to him. "Whatever happened to the theory that it was someone we don't know? Like an obsessed fan?"

"We haven't ruled that out. In fact it's still the most logical possibility. But in the meantime it only makes sense to check in our own backyards in the event that theory is wrong."

Still resistant but resolved to see it through, she conceded his point. "Okay. So who else have you got on your list?"

Again he looked distinctly uncomfortable. "That's where you come in. Tom wants the names of every man you've met since you moved to San Diego."

"You've got to be kidding."

His raised brows told her he wasn't.

She blinked slowly, drew a deep breath, then took stock. One man came immediately to mind. A photographer who saw too much, who captured too much on film. "Start with Kent Newman."

Tony's head came up. "Newman?" He frowned. "Is there something I need to know?"

She shook her head. "No. There's . . . I don't know. There's just something about him that makes me uneasy is all. Don't ask me what it is. It's just a feeling. Those deep, penetrating, artsy blue eyes of his, or something."

She shivered. "Lord, would you listen to me? Next thing you know I'll be suspecting poor Kyle, or our own Fat Man, Dan Brannigan. Oh, yes. By all means, let's add Dan to the list. We wouldn't want anyone to feel left out. I'm sure his wife would be delighted to know we suspect her husband and the father-to-be of her baby of being a stalker."

She spun around, hating this, hating herself for so easily leaning toward a loss of control.

"Hey." Tony gripped her shoulders from behind. "I know. It's awful. And it's ugly. But when it's over, and it will be over, we'll be able to put it all behind us.

"Come on. Let's finish the list. We can still get it over to Tom today. And then we have to get ready for our big night tonight."

For a few blessed moments she'd forgotten about tonight. He must have sensed her tension, because he wrapped his forearm around her upper chest and drew her back against him. "If you're not up to it, we can always call it off."

"No." She leaned into him, absorbing his strength. "I want to do it. If it means the possibility of bringing this to a head, I want to do it and get it over with."

"Good girl." He squeezed her hard. "Why don't you go get dressed. We can finish the list in the car on the way to see Tom."

She nodded, and Tony watched as Jessie squared her shoulders and walked into the house.

Sitting back down at the patio table, he slouched in the chair, stroking his jaw and wondering if he'd done the right thing.

He didn't like keeping things from Jessie. Still, he hadn't been able to bear the thought of knowing what the rest of the information Tom had given him would do to her.

Things were heating up. Tony had been right on the money with his plan to get in this guy's face and force his hand. It was working. Jessie didn't know it, but the Antony and Cleopatra billboard had gone up yesterday. And it had riled their unknown predator beyond reason.

Her friend Steven wasn't the only one who had left a message on her answering machine last night. On the heels of his message had been several other calls, all from their unknown stalker.

Tony had to believe he'd done the right thing by not telling Jessie about those calls. He had to believe that it was better that she didn't know that their "friend" had called twenty times last night, leaving one cryptic message after another. With each call his anger had escalated. With each call his threats to hurt both of them had grown more graphic.

But it was the final call that ate at Tony's gut, that filled his chest with white-hot rage.

In that call the stalker had taken great delight in describing how, with Tony looking on, he intended to take care of Jessie first, before he turned his knife on Tony.

The crush of bodies was tremendous. Hundreds of people had turned out for the unveiling of Into the Night, the new nightspot that had borrowed its name from Tony and Jessie's show.

Whether the people had come because of the nightclub itself or because of the chance to see the Falcon and the Fox in person, or both, the owners neither knew nor cared. They were ecstatic over the opening-night success.

Sequins and satin, glamour and glitter, funk and feathers, covered the bodies that danced to the sultry strains of a song by a local band, Night Moves, whose popularity in the Mission Bay area had also added to the success of the evening.

Multiple levels of shifting shadows and glitzy light treatment alternately hid and highlighted the couples swaying hip to hip, shoulder to shoulder, on the cramped quarters of half a dozen dance floors.

Tony was sticking to Jessie like glue. No mean feat, given the gyrating bodies and the demand for their attention that tugged them first one way and then the other. Even though his motive was to protect her, given the way she looked that night, he'd prefer to be chained to her anyway.

Her dress was short, black, and backless, a slinky satin sheath that left not only her back but her shoulders bare and hugged her slim shape like a body stocking. And she'd done something extraordinary to her hair, something special, something wonderfully sexy. She'd swept it up onto her head and allowed sassy, frothy curls to spill over one eye. His fingers itched to add to the artful disarray.

"Does the word *ravish* lend any specific perspective to what I have in mind for you when I get you home tonight?" he murmured into her ear as they swayed together on one of the dance floors. It was a rare moment of downtime. All evening Brian had been herding them onto the stage either to promote the station or to introduce the next set for the band or to sign eight-by-ten glossies of both the Scarlett and Rhett and the Antony and Cleopatra publicity photos.

Though she was tense and on edge, the smile she gave him was warm and intimate. "You're the one who'd better beware. Since I set eyes on you in that tux, I've only had one thought in mind."

"Which is?"

"Getting you out of it."

He laughed and, drawing her closer, spun them in a quick circle. "I've died and gone to heaven. I've had the good sense to find a multi-orgasmic woman who loves making love as much as I do."

Even in the dim lights he knew he'd managed to make her blush again.

"In spite of everything," he said, shouting to be heard above the roar when the band slammed into a heavy-metal rock number, "I'm having a good time."

"Me too," she shouted back.

The night had been intense, to say the least. While publicity for both the station and the new club was the pretense for their appearance, the underlying reason was to draw out their friend, Mr. Stalker.

Jessie had objected to the plan at first, but between Tony and Tom, she had become convinced it was worth a shot. And while not entirely comfortable with the plan himself because of the potential danger to Jess, Tony couldn't argue with its merit.

Tony, not Jessie, was the stalker's main target. The general consensus was that if anyone was in danger of an attack, it was Tony. He figured he could handle himself. The knowledge that there were at least five undercover cops at the nightclub watching over them reassured him of Jessie's safety.

As dozens of people gyrated wildly around them, he held her close, hoping their man was there somewhere, watching, steaming, getting angrier by the moment, spurring him to make a move.

Come and get me, you sorry son of a bitch, he challenged silently as he nuzzled Jessie's neck. It was partly a taunt to his unknown nemesis, partly because he couldn't get enough of her. He ran his hands in an intimate, familiar caress along her back, down her hips, swaying suggestively with her to the pounding pulse of the music. *She's mine*, his proprietary actions said. *You want me out of the way? Make your move, you demented bastard, so that my lady and I can get on with our lives.*

Jessie lifted her head from his shoulder, fanned herself in pantomime to relay that she was warm, then motioned toward one of the many exits. "I think I need a breather."

He nodded and, taking her hand in his, started leading her toward the closest door.

The mass of bodies was tremendous, the noise deafening. Working his way off the dance floor, Tony fought to keep from being separated from her. The boisterous, partying crowd closed in on them, though, and before he knew it, he'd lost hold of her hand.

He turned back to wait for her to catch up, but the horde of moving bodies drove a larger wedge between them. Helplessly stalled, he watched as she was swept into the current, forced back away from him.

"Jess," he yelled above the din. He reached for her, only to be bumped from the side and pushed farther away. Intermittently spotlighted by the flashing colored lights, she drifted into the throng of bodies, then he lost track of her completely.

"Jess!" he yelled again, trying to spot her as he tunneled his way back through the crowd.

Five minutes later he was in a panic. She was gone.

"Son of a bitch," he swore, searching, straining,

shoving people aside. Panic escalated to a fierce, gripping fear for her.

He couldn't spot her. He *had* to find her. And deep in his gut he knew he had to find her soon.

"What happened?"

He spun around.

Tom stood behind him, frowning.

"I lost her. Dammit, Tom, I lost her."

Tom pulled a transmitter out of his pocket. After uttering clipped, distinct instructions into the device, he pocketed it and turned back to Tony.

"Don't overreact." He yelled to be heard as the crowd roared their approval when the band segued into a bump-and-grind version of an old Springsteen standard.

"She probably just made her way to the lady's room," Tom continued as Tony bent down to hear him. "I've got five guys covering tonight. Every one of them is looking for her right now. Come on. Let's go check out the alley in back of the club."

Like an icebreaker parting the Arctic Ocean, Tony shouldered his way through the crowd at a slow but unrelenting pace. Tom followed in his wake, reaching out to steady a cocktail waitress when Tony bumped into her, nearly upending her and her tray of drinks in his single-minded urgency to find Jessie.

"Take it easy, man." Tom clutched Tony's arm, trying to slow him down when they reached the exit.

"Not until I find her."

"And a hell of a lot of good you'll do her with a knife parting your ribs," he yelled, slamming himself between Tony and the door. "Think! You don't know what's waiting out there. Now, slow the hell down." He drew his gun from the shoulder holster hidden under his jacket. "We'll find her. But we'll do it my way."

Until he'd seen the gun, Tony had been propelled by blind panic, insulated by a nightmarish sense of suspended reality. The sight of the gun, cold steel and deadly serious, drove home a very real message. Tom felt he might have to use it. That was as real as it got.

It wasn't just his own adrenaline rush telling him that Jessie was in danger. Tom knew it too. And they both knew she wasn't going to pop out of the lady's room with a smile on her face and say, "Hey, am I glad to see you."

He'd promised her nothing would happen to her —and now she was alone and unprotected.

Fear for her shot through Tony's bloodstream like a flash fire. Drawing on all the inner strength he possessed, he banked a surge of animal rage at what could be happening to her.

He nodded at Tom. "I'm okay. Just help me find her."

Tom put his shoulder to the door, slowly turned the handle, and eased it open a crack.

He poked his head out first, then the gun, and after looking around, slipped outside, motioning Tony to follow.

Fresh, cool air hit Tony full in the face. Cool air

and silence. Both should have cleared his head. Neither did.

The stark blackness of the night added to his sense of urgency. The deathly silence added to his sense of dread.

She'd been out of his sight too long. She'd been out of his reach too long. And she was as vulnerable to attack as the mosquito he slapped roughly from the side of his neck.

He saw nothing. No one. No movement. No sound but the echo of music bleeding eerily into the night as the door closed behind them.

"You look that way." Tom gave Tony a nudge, then started off in the opposite direction. "If you see anything, sing out, then wait for me."

His heart slamming against his ribs like a hammer, Tony searched the shadowy darkness for something he didn't want to find, was afraid not to see. He hadn't taken two steps when the crash of metal against pavement rang in the ghostly stillness, engulfing him.

Thinking only of Jessie, he bolted in the direction of the sound. At the last moment he saw the trash can rolling drunkenly toward him. He hurdled it in one long leap and hit the pavement running. The second can caught him off guard, tripping him as his foot hit it midair.

He fell face first, slamming to the pavement with a groan as his bad shoulder took the brunt of the fall. Pain lanced through his head where he grazed his temple.

Intent on only one thing, he rolled to all fours and shook the cobwebs out of his head. When his vision cleared, he looked around for any sign of Jessie. What he found sent him into a wild rage.

In a darkness illuminated by only a streetlight half a block away, the shadows shifted, then regrouped to form the silhouette of a man. And a woman.

Jessie.

She was slumped against the wall of the building. Above her a man stood as if stunned, a brick clenched in his hand. Beside her another man lay sprawled face first in the filth and debris of the alley.

"Jessie!" Tony roared, and bolted toward her.

Startled by the sound of his voice, the man holding the brick spun around to face him.

Tony froze. "Brian?"

Looking dazed, Brian sagged against the building, his breath escaping in a long, ragged moan.

"Brian, what the hell's going on here?"

Brian looked from the man lying on the pavement to the brick in his hand, then stumbled when Tony shoved him out of the way to get to Jessie.

"He—he was hurting her."

Vaguely aware of the commotion as Tom and his men arrived, Tony cradled Jessie in his arms, checking her pulse with a shaking hand, breathing a sigh of relief when he found it slow but steady.

He checked her all over for injuries. Thanking God when he found none, he tried to rouse her. "Jess. Baby. Wake up."

"Chloroform," he heard Tom say as he hunkered

down beside them, a gauze pad dangling from his fingers. "Found it a few feet away."

Jessie stirred drowsily in Tony's arms.

"She okay?"

Tony glanced up at Tom, then back at Jess, stroking her face, willing her to wake up. "I think so. I can't believe I let that son of a bitch get his hands on her."

"Well," Tom said, nodding toward the prostrate form, "he's not going to get her again. And you can thank your man here that the worst she's going to come out of this with is a headache."

Tony glanced toward a still-shaken Brian just as a police car, its siren wailing, pulled into the alley.

"Close as I can gather," Tom began, reading the questions in Tony's eyes, "Brian slipped out for a little air, saw this guy manhandling Jessie, and slick as you please, snuck up behind him and blasted him over the head with a brick." Tom chuckled. "I don't think he's quite over the shock of it."

Jessie moaned, then started struggling wildly in Tony's arms. He bit back a groan of pain as his shoulder protested at the rough treatment.

"Shhh, babe. It's okay. I've got you. Tony's got you."

Her eyes slammed open. She looked frantically around, then focused on Tony's face. "Tony . . . Oh, God, Tony. He—"

"Shhh. I know. He can't hurt you anymore."

"We got separated," she murmured sluggishly, then winced as if remembering was painful. "I . . . I waited for you by the door. But . . . when you didn't come, I just . . . I just stepped outside for a minute . . . to . . . to get some air.

"Someone grabbed me . . . and . . . and he put something o-over my face. Tony . . ." She clutched his arm, her nails digging into his flesh through his jacket.

"It's okay, Jess. You're okay now. We've got him. Actually Brian got him."

Tony glanced over her head toward the police car. Brian was leaning against it for support, haltingly repeating the story he'd told Tom of the rescue.

Turning back to Jessie as an ambulance flooded the alley with light and an insistent wailing, he asked her if she could stand up.

She took stock, then nodded.

Grimacing as fresh pain shot through his shoulder, Tony rose and helped her to her feet.

"We've got an ID on our man here," Tom said, walking back to them. He looked from Tony to Jessie. "I'm sorry, Jessie. It's Steven Hall."

"Steven?" Her voice was a reedy whisper as her gaze swung to the limp figure the paramedics were lifting onto a stretcher.

"Steven," she repeated, looking lost and confused. "Why . . . I don't understand. What's he doing here? And why would he do this?"

Tony steadied her when she swayed against him.

"Is he . . ." She clung to Tony's arm, oblivious to his wince of pain. "Is he going to be all right?"

Tom shrugged. "He took a hell of a hit. Lost a lot

of blood. He'll probably be out for a few hours, but my guess is he'll come out of it."

"Enough, Jess," Tony said, shielding her against him. "We can get the details later. Right now we need to get you to a hospital."

"I don't need a hospital."

Wrong, Tony thought. She was deathly pale and shaking violently, but he didn't want to put any more pressure on her. "Okay," he said, switching to a tactic he knew would accomplish his goal. "Then we need to get *me* to a hospital."

For the first time since she'd come to, she looked at him. Really looked at him.

"Oh, my God. You're bleeding."

He touched a hand to his temple and felt the stickiness of his own blood. "Yeah, well, you know me. Once a grandstander—"

"Quiet, Falcone," she ordered, and on shaking legs walked him in the direction of the waiting ambulance. "You need medical attention."

"I love it when you get rough with me," he murmured against her hair as he slung his good arm around her shoulders.

When they reached Brian, they stopped. With effort Tony untangled himself from Jessie and extended his hand. "I owe you, man."

Jessie touched Brian's arm, then hugged him. "We both do."

"Go get yourselves taken care of," Brian said, his discomfort over all the attention evident. "I'll check with you tomorrow."

Tomorrow.

The word echoed, wooed, consoled.

Tomorrow.

For the first time since this ugly business had started, they could look toward tomorrow without uncertainty.

Without fear.

With each other.

Tucking Jessie back under his arm, Tony contemplated the thought of tomorrow with an anticipatory pleasure that stole the brunt of the pain from his aching shoulder.

It was over.

ELEVEN

The discharge instructions from the emergency-room doctor were specific. Tony was to keep his arm in a sling until his collarbone, which had been dislocated in the fall, had a chance to mend. Jessie was to change the bandage on his temple daily and see that he wasn't a stubborn fool about not taking pain medication.

The medication was as much to ensure healing as it was to offer relief. At three-thirty that morning, however, Tony's collarbone and the scrape on his head weren't his greatest source of pain. The look on Jessie's face was. That and her silence.

After the police car delivered them to Tony's house, they walked in strained silence up his driveway. Tony leaned wearily against the side of the house as Jessie fit the key in the lock.

"How we doing?" she asked, swinging the door

open, then turning back to him with a frown of concern.

He grunted, working hard on a smile. They'd given him a potent narcotic at the hospital to take care of the intense pain of having his collarbone set. Still groggy from the lingering effects of that shot, he stumbled into the house. "We're doing great."

"Liar," she accused tenderly.

"But a wounded liar. I read somewhere that that makes it all right."

What wasn't all right, he thought, was Jessie. She was still recovering from the chloroform. She was also concerned about him. But the haunted look in her eyes spoke of the deeper source of her distress.

Tom's information on Steven Hall had been hard for Jessie to accept, the conclusion even harder.

"We ran a check on Hall this afternoon," Tom had told her as the three of them waited for the ER staff to treat Tony. "It seems he recently moved out here."

"Moved? To San Diego?" Her voice had broken when she'd followed up with a disbelieving "When?"

Tom had looked at Tony for permission. At his reluctant nod, Tom turned back to Jessie. "About the same time the calls started. Jessie, what don't we know here?"

Haltingly she told them about her friendship with Steven, his marriage proposal, and his disappointment when she'd turned him down. The picture, when fully painted, meshed conjecture with motive.

Jessie hadn't wanted to see it even as her words pulled everything together. But it was all there.

Steven Hall was a man who had evidently crossed over a line from love for a woman to maniacal obsession. Everything pointed toward a man despondent over Jessie's refusal of his marriage proposal, a man who had quit his job and followed her to San Diego, intent on winning her. No matter what the cost.

As she talked, Tony had seen how her heart refused to believe what her mind kept telling her was true. Yet Steven's attack hung over it all. Brutal, ugly, unavoidably real.

Even now, though, several hours later, Tony could see in her eyes that she was still having trouble accepting it.

"We'll make sure he gets help, Jess," he promised, leaning against the kitchen counter to keep from keeling over. Unspoken was the *if* that qualified that statement. *If* Steven Hall recovered from the blow to his head, they'd see to it that he got help.

She looked surprised at first, then grateful that he'd read her thoughts so well. "Thank you. Thank you for thinking of Steven." She shook her head, past denial but not yet embracing the truth. "I wish I understood. I don't know if I'll ever understand what happened to him to make him do this. He was always so solid, so steady. And he was my friend. Somehow I must have let him down."

"We can't be responsible for other people's actions, Jess."

She nodded. "And we can sort it out in the morning. You need to be in bed."

"Only if you tuck me in." He played for a smile and was relieved when he got a small one.

"You're just saying that because you know you can't do it yourself."

"I'm just saying that because I so fully appreciate your bedside manner."

"Come on, tough guy. I've seen enough macho from you tonight to last a lifetime. You're hurting and you're about to pass out on me."

He nuzzled her neck as she took his weight and walked him slowly toward the bedroom. "Not what you'd call a great date, huh?"

He stopped in the middle of the living room, his dark eyes somber as he looked down on her. "I couldn't have handled it, Jess. I couldn't have handled it if I'd lost you."

"You didn't lose me."

"But I could have. I didn't protect you. Hell . . ." His eyes searched her face, her disheveled hair, the rip in her nylons and the smudges of dirt on her dress. She looked so small and vulnerable as she stood there, lost in the tuxedo jacket he'd thrown over her shoulders to warm her. Suddenly he felt as guilty as the man who had done this to her. "I didn't even save you. It took Brian to do that."

She touched his face. Her hand was still cold as it drifted down to his chest and tunneled under his open shirt to rest against his bare skin. "That's where you're wrong. You saved me, Tony. Before tonight ever happened. You saved me from a bleak and very empty future without you."

The moment promised too much emotion, something neither of them could handle more of that night. To combat it, she gave him an overly bright grin. "What more could a girl ask for?"

He understood the plea in her eyes. Still, he couldn't stop the words. "I love you."

Her eyes misted over with tears. With great effort she blinked them back. "I know." She squeezed him hard and pulled herself together. "Now, walk, tough guy. I can't hold you up much longer, and something tells me you're not long for the world of the conscious."

He stumbled, losing his battle to fight off the soporific effects of the painkiller, and steadied himself with a hand on the sofa. "You've got a good point there."

"This is all so very touching."

As one they spun around to the voice.

As one they breathed a sign of relief when they saw who was standing behind them in the kitchen doorway.

"Brian." Fighting dizziness, pleased to see his friend, yet puzzled to find him there, Tony tightened his hold on Jessie. "We didn't hear you come in."

"You weren't supposed to."

It was then that Tony saw the knife . . . the dazzling silver gleam of a blade out of place and out of sync with the muzzy shadows flirting with his vision and the disconcerting taste of alarm on his tongue.

"Brian . . ." With concentrated effort he shoved Jessie behind him. "What's going on?"

Eyes narrowed, his expression grim, Brian shook his head. Sadly. Contemptuously. "Your friend made a big mistake tonight," he said, glaring at Jessie. "He got in my way. I wish I could say I was sorry about that. But he had to go. He was interfering."

"Steven?" Jessie whispered, disbelieving. "You're talking about Steven?"

"Was that his name?"

Tony fought the blurred vision and the confusion muddying his thought processes. "Brian . . . you're not making any sense."

"And you are both so gullible," he spat. "It wasn't your friend who attacked you in the alley, Jessie.

"Very good," he said with satisfaction when he saw that they finally comprehended what he'd just revealed. "For him it was a question of being in the wrong place at the wrong time. He was desperate to help you, you know. No matter. He interfered and became a casualty along the way.

"Does that thrill you?" His eyes darkened as he toyed with the knife, sliding it lovingly along his palm, tracing the length of his fingers with the tip of the blade. "Does it thrill you to know that so many men want you? Yes, I think it does. It thrills you . . . but it saddens me. You're not the person I once thought you were, Jessie."

Watching her face, he seemed lost somehow, in his own thoughts, in his own fractured code of honor. "Once, I thought you were different. But you're not. And that's what I can't forgive you for."

Though aware of imminent danger, Tony was having difficulty connecting what he was seeing and hearing to the man—the friend—who stood before him. "Brian, what the hell are you talking about?"

As sharp as broken glass, Brian's gaze cut to Tony. "What am I talking about? I'm talking about betrayal. I'm talking about broken promises."

"Promises?" Jessie said, her voice thin with rising fear.

"Promises," Brian repeated, walking slowly toward them. "You made promises, Jessie. You know you did," he insisted when she shook her head. "With your smile. With your kindness. You were attracted to me. No, it won't do any good to deny it. I saw. I knew."

With a harsh laugh he turned back to Tony. "But you . . . Why couldn't you have left her alone?" The laughter faded, rage a stark and stunning replacement. "Why, just once, couldn't you have considered a woman off-limits and backed the hell away?

"You made rules, for God's sake," he continued accusingly, not even aware that he had cut his thumb with his knife. Blood, crimson red, dripping like teardrops, wept from the tip of his finger.

"No office romances, you said. Not good for business, you said. Not good for revenue." He snorted, outraged. "Did you ever once stop to think you were breaking your own rule? Did you ever stop to think that finally, because of your rule, *I* might want something for myself? Something Tony Falcone hadn't ever had?"

Tony felt Jessie's grip on his arm tighten. Felt the trembling as she accepted that the nightmare they'd thought was over had barely begun.

"Oh, God," she whispered. "All the time . . . The calls, everything . . . it was you."

Brian laughed again. Without humor. With bitter malice and completely beyond reason. "From the beginning I thought you were special. And you were so nice to me. Why were you so nice to me if you were only interested in him?"

She made to move toward him. "Brian, we can talk about this." Tony gripped her arm and held her back.

"What's to talk about?" Brian said brightly. "You had your chance. Even if I didn't have mine. Not yet anyway," he added with a look that turned Tony's blood to ice. An ugly and rapidly encroaching realization of where this was heading gripped him.

"I was finally going to have it my way earlier tonight. If that friend of yours hadn't stumbled onto us in the alley. I had it all planned. I was going to make you see. I was going to give you a chance to see that it should be me. Not him," he added, glaring at Tony.

He motioned with the knife. "Over here."

They stood motionless, still too stunned to believe what was happening. A friend transformed before their eyes to an enemy. A kind and gentle spirit reduced by a twisted sense of reality to a demented and unreasonable danger.

Tony hurt with a sense of loss that went beyond grief. He knew what he had to do to get Jessie out of this unharmed. Steeling himself, he blocked the memories of years of friendship and prepared to defend her against the man who stood before them.

The disconnected look in Brian's eyes was eerie and frightening as he walked to where they stood, the blade clutched loosely, almost lovingly in his bleeding hand.

He smiled, then with a lightning move that took them both by surprise, he slammed a fist into Tony's dislocated shoulder.

Tony doubled over in pain, and Brian took instant advantage. He grabbed Jessie and dragged her against him as he rammed a knee up into Tony's face. Tony crumpled in a heap on the carpet.

"Tony!" Jessie screamed. She fought to pull away from Brian, but his grip on her arm was punishing and strong. He shoved her into a chair, then snagging a fistful of her hair, sat down on the chair's arm above her, the knife tucked deadly and snug against her throat.

"What's the matter, friend?" he asked, sounding pleased and contemptuous as he watched Tony struggle to sit up. "Doesn't it feel great coming in last? Doesn't it feel victorious knowing you aren't going to win this round?"

Grimacing in pain, Tony sucked in air. He slumped back against the sofa, clutching his bad shoulder, tasting the blood flowing from his split lip. "I thought we were friends. Friends talk. We . . . we could have worked this through. We still can."

"When did we ever talk anything through? When did you ever give anything but orders and I jumped to your tune like one of Pavlov's dogs?"

"Is that the way you saw it?" Tony asked, groaning as he pulled himself up straighter.

"It wasn't the way I *saw* it. It's the way it *was*. Always. From the time we met in college—"

"We were friends," Tony insisted, fighting to see his way through this. Trying to battle the pain and the medication and find an opening to get Jessie away from Brian.

"We were never friends," Brian spat. "*You* had the friends. I was just your shadow. Always *in* your shadow. No one ever knew I existed." He tightened his grip on Jessie's hair. She cried out as he jerked her head back, forcing her to look at him. "Until Jessie came along. She was nice to me. She was a friend to me. She was even attracted to me—until you started pouring on the charm. You've got it to spare, haven't you, Falcone?"

Tony clenched his jaw, digging deep for control as he watched Brian manhandle Jessie. The knife was too close. Brian was too far gone. His only hope was to keep Brian talking until he saw his chance.

He'd only get one shot. It had to be a good one because he seriously doubted he'd have the strength to survive a prolonged struggle.

"I don't understand you, Brian," he said as he

shifted his weight onto his hip. He winced sharply, overplaying the pain in an attempt to boost Brian's confidence that he was out of commission. "If you were attracted to Jessie, why didn't you tell me? And if you wanted her for yourself, why did you keep throwing us together for those billboard shots?"

It was exactly the wrong question to ask. Anger flared in Brian's eyes, and he knotted his fist tighter in Jessie's hair. She flinched and stiffened in an attempt to escape the bite of the blade riding so dangerously close to her jugular.

"Why? Because I was testing you. Testing both of you." He looked down at Jessie, his eyes sad suddenly, tempered with a tenderness that contradicted the razor-edged knife at her throat. "I was giving you a chance to back away from each other, to resist the temptation. But you failed the test. You failed miserably. And now you have to pay the price."

"It's me you want to hurt, Brian," Tony said quickly, inching a little higher. "Not her. She hasn't done anything to you."

Brian nodded, drew a shuddering breath, then met Tony's eyes. "And that's what's so sad. Because of you she has to pay too. Remember that when you watch me hurt her. And remember that you had to sit there, too weak to do anything about it."

"That's where you're wrong, Brian," Tony said, forcing himself to speak slowly, steadily, and to keep his gaze trained on Brian, not on Tut, who had just sidled into the room. "You won't hurt her. You don't really want to. And I can't let you."

"You can't stop me."

New hope flared in Tony's chest as the big Siamese, oblivious to the drama taking place, sized up the occupants of the room and focused on the one individual who was not familiar to him.

"You can't think you can get away with this," Tony said. He fought to maintain eye contact with Brian while in his peripheral vision he saw Tut stalk closer, pause, sit, then lick his paw at a maddeningly leisurely pace. "I can't imagine why you'd want to," he continued as a cold sweat broke out on his forehead. "You've already outsmarted us."

"You never knew, did you?" Brian said, pride in his cleverness taking priority over his final plan. "I had you all fooled."

Jessie cringed as the knife pressed harder against her throat. Tony read the fear in her eyes, but thanked God she remained calm, taking her cue from him. The seconds ticked by, each one an hour.

"How did you disguise your voice?" Tony asked, still playing for time.

"That was the easy part," Brian said, gloating over his victory. "You should have been able to figure that out. A small device over the receiver did the trick."

Now, Tut now, Tony pleaded silently as he swallowed and forced himself to keep talking.

"You're right," he agreed. He gathered his strength as Tut stood, stared, then snapped his tail in a telling twitch.

Do it, do it, Tony willed the cat. He held his

breath as Tut poised in a crouch that could only mean one thing.

Quicker than the eye could follow, the cat sprang from the floor to the chair. He landed with a yowl and a thud, directly on Brian's lap.

The second of startled reaction was all the time Tony needed. With a roar that sent Tut scampering and Jessie diving for the floor, Tony lunged at Brian. The force of the blow hurled them over backward in the chair. Tony landed on top of Brian with all his weight, knocking the wind out of him.

Gasping for air, struggling beneath Tony, Brian flailed wildly as they rolled across the floor. The knife sliced through the air, coming dangerously close to connecting with Tony's back.

"Run, Jessie. Run!" Tony shouted as he fought not only the consuming pain in his shoulder but the dizziness that sucked him toward unconsciousness.

In the distance, in a far-off somewhere, disconnected from the reality and the rage and the blinding force that kept him conscious and fighting Brian, he heard the wail of a siren.

Too late to stop the fiery bite of the blade into his back.

Too late to stop the explosion of pain and the sickening haze of weakness that engulfed him.

Another sound . . . A roar—his own—split the air as with a final surge of adrenaline, he reared up. He had to protect her. Had to . . . protect her . . .

Blood streamed from his arm as he slammed his fist into Brian's face . . . again . . . and again, until with a low groan he slumped across Brian's supine body.

He felt as much as heard his own breath, choppy and labored and strangely hissing, as it beat across the pummeled face of the man he had considered a friend.

The echoing sound of Jessie's scream rang in his ears as the blackness defeated him.

TWELVE

"What a guy won't do to get a little attention."

Tony heard her voice as if from a distance. He fought past the haze and a pain that was both pleasantly disconnected and achingly real, struggling to open his eyes. When he saw Jessie, it was all worth the effort. "Hey, Jess."

"Hey yourself," she said softly, her voice laced with both gladness and tears. "You took your sweet time about coming around, you big Italian grandstander."

Another smile, this one his, was followed by a grimace. "If I'd known it was going to hurt this much, I'd have made it a point to stay under a little longer."

She pressed a hand to his cheek. "Then go back to sleep. Now that I know you're okay, we'll have plenty of time to talk later."

He groped for her hand. "You're okay?"

She squeezed it tightly. "I'm fine. Thanks to you. And Tut."

Tut. It took a moment to understand her remark. His eyes drifted closed, a smile playing at one corner of his mouth. "I knew I kept that arrogant feline around for a reason."

The hospital kept Tony around for a reason too. Besides reinjuring his shoulder, Brian's knife had found its mark before Tony had disabled him. They kept him a full ten days before they let Jessie bring him home. It was none too soon, as far as Tony was concerned. He hadn't exactly been a model patient.

"You ought to be ashamed of yourself," Jessie scolded as she helped him through the kitchen. "They were just doing their jobs."

"With great relish, I might add," he grumbled. "They didn't have to enjoy it so much."

"Well, now it's my turn to enjoy it." Walking him slowly toward the bedroom, she made sure he knew who was in charge. "You've been up long enough."

"Do you believe this?" He appealed to Sarah for help. "She's turned into Attila the Nightingale."

Sarah grinned and, juggling two huge bouquets of flowers, led the way to the bedroom. "Don't get me into the middle of this. I'm just along for moral support."

Despite his grousing and grumbling, he was pale and still weak. But Jessie knew he was going to be all right. There was a time when they'd thought he might not be.

Brian's wild thrashing had almost proven deadly for Tony. Aside from the tremendous blood loss from the stab wound, the knife had punctured a lung.

Jessie refused to let herself think about it as she and Sarah settled Tony into bed. The fact that he fell asleep shortly after they'd drawn the drapes told of his diminished strength.

Over coffee on the patio mother and daughter sat in a comfortable silence under a California sun that seemed a promise of brighter days ahead.

Relieved that Tony was finally out of the hospital, Jessie took a moment to reflect on everything that had happened. Sometimes it was still too much to accept. She shuddered to think how differently it could have all turned out if Steven hadn't regained consciousness when he had and if Tom hadn't dispatched a cruiser to check on Tony's house. The officers had arrived just as Tony passed out.

"It's okay, Mom," Sarah said, her eyes probing and concerned. "It's over. Finally."

Jessie drew a deep breath. "I know, sweetie. I'm sorry. Sometimes . . . sometimes it catches me off guard and I can't stop the memories—and the fears—from creeping back in."

"I wish you'd told me about what was going on from the beginning."

Jessie shook her head. "Of all the things that happened, that's one I would never change. There was nothing you could have done. And there was no need for you to be frightened too."

Sarah was silent for a moment, conceding the point, then she shrugged. "I still don't understand how Steven Hall ended up in the middle of this. You said he moved out here?"

Jessie nodded. "Just that week. He'd gotten a promotion and his company had transferred him to the Mission Bay area. He'd tried to call me when he got settled, but hadn't been able to catch up with me. When he saw the advertisement for the opening of Into the Night and realized I'd be there, he decided to surprise me."

"Surprise," Sarah echoed, the word encompassing the full, disastrous range of the surprise Steven had run into.

"Yeah," Jessie agreed regretfully. "Some surprise."

Steven was okay. Thank God. Jessie had had several opportunities to speak with him since the night of the attacks. So had the police. It was because Steven had regained consciousness shortly after she and Tony had been released from the emergency room that Tony was alive right now. Woozy from the concussion but coherent enough to make sense, Steven had relayed his innocence to Tom Wayfield, who had stayed behind to question him on the off chance that he would come to.

Tom's experience, good instincts, and solid judgment convinced him to believe Steven when he told

Tom that Brian had been attacking Jessie and that Steven had intervened.

Steven's role was nothing short of extraordinary, a huge accident of fate that had brought him to the club that night and then landed him in the hospital.

"You going to be okay if I head back to campus?" Sarah asked, breaking into her thoughts.

Jessie smiled. "I'm going to be fine. Thanks, sweetie. For being here. And for . . ." She hesitated, then began again. "For being so accepting about Tony."

"You mean about Tony and you," Sarah clarified, smiling. "He's a great guy, Mom."

"And it doesn't bother you?"

Sarah looked away, considering. "Maybe at first, I guess it did. But I think it was more because I was still having trouble letting go of the idea of you and Dad getting back together." She paused, then gave her mother that adult, conspiratorial grin that was new to Jessie and that she loved so much. "Besides, this is the nineties. What's a few years' difference between friends? If you love him and he loves you, then that's what matters. And he does love you, Mom. He couldn't make that any clearer. Someday I hope the man I love will look at me like that."

They both turned at a sound rumbling from the general direction of Tony's bedroom.

Jessie grinned. "Sounds like the man who loves me just bellowed. Bless him, he does not do convalescence well."

"You'd better go see what he needs." Sarah hugged her mother hard, then headed for her car. "And see to it that that cat gets all the attention he needs too."

Tut was getting plenty of attention these days. While Jessie still hadn't won him over completely, she was his slave for life. Wild as it seemed, if it hadn't been for Tut, neither she nor Tony might have lived to consider which commercial endorsement to accept on behalf of the feline celebrity. The newspapers were having a field day with the story of the Siamese's role in the rescue.

Pausing outside Tony's bedroom door, Jessie was content just to watch him. She was happy beyond measure to see him back in his bed, even though he was staring broodily out the window. His physical wounds would heal. So would his emotional ones, though they might take a little longer.

"How's it going?"

He turned at the sound of her voice, his scowl softening marginally. "I hate this."

She moved to the bed and eased a hip onto the mattress beside him. "I know."

"And I hate being patronized."

She patted his hand, biting back a grin. "I know that too."

He gave her the evil eye. "I will get even, you know. When I have my cursed strength back, you're going to pay for all those bed baths and bedpans, those breezy hospital gowns, those long, dull needles that you stood by and watched people poke into my buns."

"They're such nice buns," she said, commiserating more with the nursing staff than with him. "I couldn't blame them for wanting to see them as often as possible."

"You're really pushing it, you know that, don't you?"

Undaunted, she slipped off her shoes, then carefully climbed onto the bed and eased astride him. Bracing herself on her hands and knees, she slowly lowered her face to his. "I know what you need."

His eyes never left hers as with infinite care she touched her mouth to his, then dropped tender, healing kisses to his still-bruised face. "So many places to kiss and make better," she whispered against the shoulder that had to be reset a second time after he'd wrestled Brian to the floor. "So little time."

Finally relaxing as she'd intended for him to do, he sighed, enjoying her ministrations. "You missed a spot," he murmured, pointing to the corner of his mouth. She gladly tended to it with the sweetest of kisses. "And I missed you," he added with a whispered moan as with ultimate care she let him pull her down beside him to nestle in the curve of his arm. "God, I've missed holding you like this."

She smiled against his chest. "Much as I appreciate the care you got in the hospital and the attention from your family, I have to admit I'm glad to finally have you alone and all to myself."

He ran his hand up and down her arm. His strong, even breathing beneath her ear was like music. A steady, beautiful rhythm that only days ago had been harsh and labored.

"I told you my mother would love you."

His mother, his father, all his brothers and his sister had come out in force to keep vigil, lend support, and worry over her welfare as much as they worried over Tony's.

"Your family is very special."

"That's why you'll fit in so well."

He became silent then, his hand stilling on her arm. She sensed the moment his thoughts turned to Brian.

"I still don't know how this happened," he said.

He knew, Jessie thought. He just didn't want to accept that as Brian's friend he hadn't realized Brian had a problem. Jessie knew too well the struggle Tony was waging. It was the same one she'd battled when she'd thought Steven had slipped over the edge.

More and more information about Brian and what had driven him to his obsession with her kept coming to light. His problems, it seemed, were deep-seated and an integral part of a troubled past. While the revelation that Brian had been in and out of psychiatric institutions and in and out of trouble since he was a child aided in understanding, the truth was still difficult to face.

"Mental illness is never easy to understand, Tony.

You had no way of knowing what was going on inside his head."

"I should have seen or sensed something was wrong."

"No, you shouldn't have. You couldn't have. Even his family had no idea he was having problems again. And you," she continued, knowing he was beating himself up on another count, "you were too busy being his friend to see. You trusted him; you took him at face value. And I want you to get it out of your head that you let him down. No one could have been better to Brian than you have been.

"He's getting help now," she reminded him when she felt his jaw clench against the top of her head.

"Now that it's too late."

"It may have always been too late for him. At least now he can't hurt anyone else . . . and maybe he'll find some peace for himself.

"Now, hush." She soothed a hand across his brow. "When you're better, we can talk about this. And we'll do whatever you think is best to help him. In the meantime close your eyes. Go to sleep. Just think, when you wake up, you can grouse and grumble, all rested and refreshed."

"I guess I'm not a very good patient, huh?"

"Let's put it this way . . ." She raised herself up, bracing her weight on one arm so that she could see his face. "It's a good thing I'm the one in this family who's going to bear the babies."

His eyes widened, then glittered with all the emotion he felt inside. "Ah, Jess . . . I wouldn't ask that of you."

She thought again of his family, of the adorable nieces and nephews, and the child he deserved to have, who would be as beautiful as his or her father.

"You worked so hard to convince me that age makes no difference. Don't renege on me now, Falcone. If we're going to play this out, then it's going to be to the fullest."

He was silent for a moment before he asked in a hoarse whisper, "Does this mean you're saying yes?"

She grinned. "What was the question again? Something about living with you forever and putting up with your cat?"

He chuckled, then caught himself when pain gripped him. "If I remember right, I believe it was my mother who asked you if you intended to marry me and have her grandchildren."

She sliced him an accusing look. "So you *were* awake for that."

"I was awake." He reached out and touched his fingers to the falcon that she'd worn for safekeeping and that she'd told herself kept him close until she could lie in his arms again. "I was also awake when you asked her how old I was."

"For all the good it did me. She's as tight-lipped about it as you are."

Fatigue showed through his grin as he slowly closed his eyes, his dark lashes shadowing the crest of his cheeks. "Runs in the family."

"How old *are* you, Tony?" she asked in a persuasive whisper.

"You ought to be ashamed of yourself, trying to take advantage of a man in a weak moment."

She sighed, and gave it up for the moment. "It was worth a shot."

"And it may be worth a shot to stick around. If you stay long enough, I just may clue you in."

"Okay. Play your little game if you want. I'll humor you, but I *will* find out."

"Eventually."

She laughed. "Sooner than you think. There's the little matter of the marriage license. I believe that in addition to both of our signatures it requires our birth dates."

"Well, until then, I guess you'll just have to live with the suspense."

She loved that smile. It teased and played and promised. It was the smile that had captured her heart from the beginning, and she couldn't imagine a future without it.

"I'll wait," she said, deciding it was time to let him rest. "But your nap can't. I want you back on your feet, so I think I'd better leave you alone so that you can sleep."

His arm tightened around her. "Don't go. Stay with me, Jess."

Loving him, loving the solid strength of his body beside her, she settled back down beside him. "I'll stay right here."

His arm banded tighter still. "Always. Promise you'll stay with me always."

Her heart, rich and full and strong with the love she felt, beat against his side, its rhythm as steady as time, as honest as the promise she made him. "Always."

THE EDITOR'S CORNER

What an irresistible lineup we have for you next month! These terrific romances from four of our most talented authors deliver wonderful heroines and sexy heroes. They are full of passion, fun, and intensity—just what you need to keep warm on those crisp autumn nights.

Starting things off is **ONE ENCHANTED AUTUMN, LOVESWEPT #710**, from supertalented Fayrene Preston, and enchanted is exactly how Matthew Stone feels when he meets the elegant attorney Samantha Elliott. She's the one responsible for introducing his aunt to her new beau, and wary that the beau might be a fortune hunter, Matthew is determined to stop the wedding. Samantha invites Matthew to dinner, sure that seeing the loving couple together will convince the cynical reporter, but she soon finds herself the object of Matthew's own amorous pursuit. Another utterly romantic novel of unexpected passion and exquisite sensuality from Fayrene.

Billie Green is back with **STARWALKER**, LOVESWEPT #711, a unique and sexy romance that'll have you spellbound. Born of two bloods, torn between two worlds, Marcus Aurelius Reed is arrogant, untamed—and the only man who can save Laken Murphy's brother's life. She needs a Comanche shaman to banish an unseen evil, but he refuses to help her, swears the man she seeks no longer exists. Her persistence finally pays off, but the real challenge begins when Laken agrees to share his journey into a savage past. Tempted by this lord of dark secrets, Laken must now trust him with her wild heart. Once more Billie seduces her fans with this enthralling story of true love.

Victoria Leigh gives us a heroine who only wants to be **BLACKTHORNE'S WOMAN**, LOVESWEPT #712. Micah Blackthorne always captures his quarry, but Bethany Corbett will do anything to elude her pursuer and keep her baby safe—risk her life on snowy roads, even draw a gun! But once she understands that he is her only chance for survival, she pleads for a truce and struggles to prove her innocence. Micah refuses to let his desire for the beautiful young mother interfere with his job, but his instincts tell him she is all she claims to be . . . and more. In a world of betrayal and dark desire, only he can command her surrender—and only she can possess his soul. Victoria has created a thrilling tale of heated emotions, racing pulses, and seductive passions that you won't be able to put down.

Please give a big welcome to Elaine Lakso, whose debut novel will have you in **HIGH SPIRITS**,

LOVESWEPT #713. Cody McRae is tall, dark, dangerously unpredictable—and the only man Cass MacFarland has ever loved! Now, six years after he's accused her of betrayal, she is back in town . . . and needs his help to discover if her spooky house is truly haunted. As wickedly handsome as ever, Cody bets Cass he is immune to her charms—but taking his dare might mean getting burned by the flames in his eyes. Funny, outrageous, and shamelessly sexy, this wonderful novel offers spicy suspense and two unforgettable characters whose every encounter strikes romantic sparks.

Happy reading!

With warmest wishes,

Beth de Guzman

Beth de Guzman

Senior Editor

P.S. Don't miss the women's novels coming your way in October. In the blockbuster tradition of Julie Garwood, **THIEF OF HEARTS** by Teresa Medeiros is a captivating historical romance of adventure and triumph; **VIRGIN BRIDE** by Tamara Leigh is an electrifying medieval romance in which a woman falls in love with her mortal enemy; **COURTING MISS HATTIE** by award-winning author Pamela Morsi is an unforgettable novel in which handsome Reed Tylor shares a scorching kiss with Hattie Colfax and realizes that his best friend is the only woman he will ever love. We'll be giving you a sneak peek at these wonderful books in next month's LOVESWEPTs. And immediately following this page, look for a preview of the terrific romances from Bantam that are *available now!*

Don't miss these phenomenal books by your
favorite Bantam authors

On sale in August:

THE LAST BACHELOR
by *Betina Krahn*

PRINCE OF WOLVES
by *Susan Krinard*

WHISPERED LIES
by *Christy Cohen*

"One of the genre's most creative writers. Her ingenious romances always entertain and leave readers with a warm glow."
—*Romantic Times*

Betina Krahn

THE LAST BACHELOR

Betina Krahn, author of the national bestsellers THE PRINCESS AND THE BARBARIAN and MY WARRIOR'S HEART, is one of the premier names in romance. Now, with this spectacularly entertaining battle of the sexes, her distinctive humor and charm shine brighter than ever.

Antonia's bedroom was a masterpiece of Louis XIV opulence . . . in shades of teal and seafoam and ecru, with touches of gilt, burnt umber, and apricot. Sir Geoffrey had spared no expense to see to her pleasure and her comfort: from the hand-tinted friezes on the ceilings, to the ornate floor-to-ceiling bed, to the thick Aubusson carpets, to the exquisite tile stove, hand-painted with spring flowers, he had imported from Sweden to insure the room would be evenly warm all winter. Every shape, every texture was lush and feminine, meant to delight her eye and satisfy her touch . . . the way her youth and beauty and energy had delighted her aging husband. It was her personal retreat, a balm for her spirits, her sanctuary away from the world.

And Remington Carr had invaded it.

When she arrived breathless at her chamber door, she could see that the heavy brocades at the windows had been gathered back and the south-facing windows had been thrown open to catch the sultry breeze. Her hand-painted and gilded bed was mounded with bare ticking, and her linens, comforters, and counterpane were piled in heaps on the floor around the foot of the bed. It took a moment to locate Remington.

He stood by her dressing table with his back to her, his shirt sleeves rolled up and his vest, cravat, and collar missing. The sight of his long, black-clad legs and his wide, wedge-shaped back sent a distracting shiver through her. When his head bent and his shoulder flexed, she leaned to one side to see what he was doing.

He was holding one of her short black gloves and as she watched, he brought it to his nose, closed his eyes, and breathed in. A moment later, he strolled to the nearby bench, where her shot-silk petticoat and French-cut corset—the purple satin one, covered with black Cluny lace—lay exactly as she had left them the evening before. She looked on, horrified, as he lifted and wiggled the frilly hem of her petticoat, watching the delicate flounces wrap around his wrist. Abandoning that, he ran a speculative hand over the molded cups at the top of her most elegant stays, then dragged his fingers down the front of them to toy with the suspenders that held up her stockings. She could see his smile in profile.

"No garters," he murmured, just loud enough to hear in the quiet.

"Just what do you think you are doing?" she demanded, lurching forward a step before catching herself.

He turned sharply, then relaxed into a heart-stopping smile at the sight of her.

"Women's work . . . what else?" he said in insufferably pleasant tones. "I've just given your featherbeds a sound thrashing, and I am waiting for the dust to clear so I can get on with turning your mattresses."

"My mattresses don't need turning, thank you," she charged, her face reddening. "No more than my most personal belongings need plundering. How dare you invade my bedchamber and handle my things?" She was halfway across the room before she realized he wasn't retreating, and that, in fact, the gleam in his eyes intensified as she approached, making it seem that he had been waiting for her. Warnings sounded in her better sense and she halted in the middle of the thick carpet.

"Put those back"—she pointed to the gloves in his hand—"and leave at once."

He raised one eyebrow, then glanced at the dainty black seven-button glove he held. "Only the best Swedish kid, I see. One can always tell Swedish glove leather by the musk that blends so nicely with a woman's own scent. Your scent is roses, isn't it?" He inhaled the glove's scent again and gave her a desirous look. "I do love roses."

He was teasing, flirting with her again . . . the handsome wretch. It was no good appealing to his sense of shame; where women were concerned, he didn't seem to have one. Her only hope, she realized, was to maintain her distance and her composure and use deflating candor to put him in his place. And his place, she told her racing heart, was anywhere *except* the middle of her bedroom.

"You rush headlong from one outrage into another, don't you, your lordship?" she declared, crossing her arms and resisting the hum of excitement rising in her blood. "You haven't the slightest regard for decency or propriety—"

"I do wish you would call me Remington," he said with exaggerated sincerity. "I don't think a first-name-basis would be considered too much familiarity with a man who is about to climb into your bed and turn it upside down." Trailing that flagrant double entendre behind him, he tossed her glove aside and started for the bed.

"Into my . . . ?" Before she could protest, he was indeed climbing up into the middle of her bed, pushing the featherbed to the foot of the bed and seizing the corners of the mattress. As the ropes shifted and groaned and the thick mattress began to roll, she felt a weightless sensation in the pit of her stomach and understood that he was moving more than just a cotton-stuffed ticking. The sight of him in those vulnerable confines was turning her inside out, as well.

"Come down out of there this instant, Remington Carr!" She hurried to the edge of the bed, frantic to get him out of it.

"I have a better idea," he said, shoving to his feet and bracing his legs to remain stable on the springy ropes. "Why don't you come up here? There's plenty of room." He flicked a suggestive look around him, then pinned it on her. "You know, this is a very large bed for a woman who sleeps by herself. How long has it been, Antonia, since you've had your ticking turned?"

A romance of mystery, magic,
and forbidden passion

PRINCE OF WOLVES
by
Susan Krinard

"A brilliantly talented new author."
—*Romantic Times*

Through with running from the past, Joelle Randall had come to the rugged Canadian Rockies determined to face her pain and begin anew. All she needed was a guide to lead her through the untamed mountain wilderness to the site where her parents' plane had crashed so long ago. But the only guide Joelle could find was Luke Gévaudan, a magnetically attractive loner with the feral grace of a wolf and eyes that glittered with a savage intensity. She couldn't know that Luke was the stuff of legends, one of the last survivors of an ancient race of werewolves . . . a man whose passion she would not be able to resist—no matter how terrible the price.

Joey was too lost in her own musings to immediately notice the sudden hush that fell over the bar. The absence of human chatter caught her attention slowly, and she blinked as she looked around. The noisy clumps of men were still at their tables, but they seemed almost frozen in place. Only the television, nearly drowned out before, broke the quiet.

There was a man standing just inside the doorway, as still as all the others, a silhouette in the dim light. It took Joey a moment to realize that he was the focus of this strange and vivid tableau.

Even as the thought registered, someone coughed. It broke the hush like the snap of a twig in a silent forest. The room suddenly swelled again with noise, a relieved blast of sound as things returned to normal.

Joey turned to Maggie.

"What was that all about?" she asked. Maggie was slow to answer, but the moment of gravity was short-lived, and the barkeep smiled again and shook her head.

"Sorry about that. Must have seemed pretty strange, I guess. But he tends to have that effect on people around here."

Joey leaned forward on her elbow, avoiding a wet puddle on the counter. "Who's 'he'?" she demanded, casting a quick glance over her shoulder.

Setting down the mug she'd been polishing, Maggie assumed an indifference Joey was certain she didn't feel. "His name is Luke Gévaudan. He lives some way out of town—up the slope of the valley. Owns a pretty big tract of land to the east."

Joey slewed the stool around to better watch the man, chin cupped in her hand. "I know you've said people here don't much care for outsiders," she remarked, "but you have to admit that was a pretty extreme reaction. . . . Gévaudan, you said. Isn't that a French name?"

"French-Canadian," Maggie corrected.

"So he's one of these . . . French-Canadians? Is

that why the people here don't like him?" She studied Maggie over her shoulder.

"It's not like that," Maggie sighed. "It's hard to explain to someone from outside—I mean, he's strange. People don't trust him, that's all. And as a rule he doesn't make much of an attempt to change that. He keeps to himself."

Unexpectedly intrigued, Joey divided her attention between the object of her curiosity and the redhead. "Don't kid me, Maggie. He may be strange and he may be standoffish, but you can't tell me that wasn't more than just mild distrust a minute ago."

Maggie leaned against the bar and sagged there as if in defeat. "I said it's complicated. I didn't grow up here, so I don't know the whole story, but there are things about the guy that bother people. I hear he was a strange kid." She hesitated. "He's also got a bit of a reputation as a—well, a ladykiller, I guess you could say." She grinned and tossed her red curls. "I'm not sure that's the right word. Let's put it this way—he's been known to attract the ladies, and it's caused a bit of a ruckus now and then."

"Interesting," Joey mused. "If he's so popular with the local women, I can see why the men around here wouldn't be overly amused."

"It's not just local women," Maggie broke in, falling naturally into her usual habit of cozy gossip. "Though there were a couple of incidents—before my time, you understand. But I know there've been a few outsiders who've, shall we say, taken up with him." She gave an insinuating leer. "They all left, every one of them, after a few months. And none of them ever talked."

Wondering when she'd get a clear look at his face, Joey cocked an eye at her friend. "I guess that could make for some resentment. He may be mysterious, but he doesn't sound like a very nice guy to me."

"There you go," Maggie said, pushing herself off the bar. "Consider yourself warned." She winked suggestively. "The way you're staring at him, I'd say you need the warning."

At Joey's start of protest, Maggie sashayed away to serve her customers. Joey was left to muse on what she'd been told. Not that it really mattered, in any case. She wasn't interested in men. There were times when she wondered if she ever would be again. But that just wasn't an issue now. She had far more important things on her mind. . . .

Her thoughts broke off abruptly as the man called Gévaudan turned. There was the briefest hush again, almost imperceptible; if Joey hadn't been so focused on him and what had happened, she might never have noticed. For the first time she could see him clearly as he stepped into the light.

The first impression was of power. It was as if she could see some kind of aura around the man—too strong a feeling to dismiss, as much as it went against the grain. Within a moment Joey had an instinctive grasp of why this Luke Gévaudan had such a peculiar effect on the townspeople. He seemed to be having a similar effect on her.

Her eyes slid up his lithe form, from the commonplace boots and over the snug, faded jeans that molded long, muscular legs. She skipped quickly over his midtorso and took in the expanse of chest and broad shoulders, enhanced rather than hidden by the deep green plaid of his shirt. But it was when she reached his face that the full force of that first impression hit her.

He couldn't have been called handsome—not in

that yuppified modern style represented by the clean-cut models in the ads back home. There was a rough-ness about him, but not quite the same unpolished coarseness that typified many of the local men. In-stead, there was a difference—a uniqueness—that she couldn't quite compare to anyone she'd seen before.

Her unwillingly fascinated gaze traveled over the strong, sharply cut lines of his jaw, along lips that held a hint of reserved mobility in their stillness. His nose was straight and even, the cheekbones high and hard, hollowed underneath with shadow. The hair that fell in tousled shocks over his forehead was mainly dark but liberally shot with gray, especially at the temples. The age this might have suggested was visible no-where in his face or body, though his bearing an-nounced experience. His stance was lightly poised, alert, almost coiled, like some wary creature from the wilds.

But it wasn't until she reached his eyes that it all coalesced into comprehension. They glowed. She shook her head, not sure what she was seeing. It wasn't a literal glow, she reminded herself with a last grasp at logic, but those eyes shone with their own inner light. They burned—they burned on hers. Her breath caught in her throat. He was staring at her, and for the first time she realized he was returning her examination.

She met his gaze unflinchingly for a long moment. His eyes were pale—and though in the dim light she could not make out the color, she could sense the warm light of amber in their depths. Striking, unusual eyes. Eyes that burned. Eyes that seemed never to blink but held hers in an unnerving, viselike grip. Eyes that seemed hauntingly familiar. . . .

Joey realized she was shaking when she finally

looked away. Her hands were clasped together in her lap, straining against each other with an internal struggle she was suddenly conscious of. Even now she could feel his gaze on her, intense and unwavering, but she resisted the urge to look up and meet it again. The loss of control she'd felt in those brief, endless moments of contact had been as unexpected and frightening as it was inexplicable. She wasn't eager to repeat the experience. But the small, stubborn core of her that demanded control over herself and her surroundings pricked at her without mercy. With a soft curse on an indrawn breath, Joey looked up.

He was gone.

Some secrets are too seductive to keep, and too dangerous to reveal.

WHISPERED LIES
by
Christy Cohen

For thirty-seven years Leah Shaperson had been trapped in a marriage devoid of passion. Then a stranger's tantalizing touch awakened her desires, and she found that she'd do anything to feel wanted once more . . . even submit to reckless games and her lover's darkest fantasies. But she would soon learn that the price of forbidden pleasure is steep. . . .

"I know," Elliot said. His voice was hoarse and the words were garbled.

"What?"

"I said I know," Elliot said, turning to her. He showed her a face she didn't recognize, red with suppressed rage. She clutched her nightgown to her chest.

"You know what?" she asked. She would make him say it. She still could not believe he knew. No one could know and not say anything. He had come home on time tonight and they'd had dinner together. How could he sit through a whole dinner with her and not say anything? How could he have sat through so many dinners, gotten through so many days, and still kept quiet?

Elliot stepped toward her, his face and neck blistering from rage, and Leah saw James's face in his. She saw the recklessness, the fury, the need to lash out. She stepped back, but then Elliot turned from her and lunged for the bed. He yanked the blankets off and threw them on the floor. Then he grabbed the pillows, flung them hard against the mattress, then hurled them across the room. He stared back at her, burned her with his gaze, then, in one viciously graceful move, swiped his arm across the dresser, knocking over frames and bottles of perfume. Glass shattered on the hardwood floor and liquid seeped into the wood, bombarding the room with fragrances.

Elliot looked around wildly. He started toward her and Leah jumped back, but then he turned and ran to the closet. He flung open the door and grabbed one of Leah's blouses. He ripped it off the hanger, then hurled it at her face.

Leah watched this man, this alien man, as he ripped off blouse after blouse and flung each one at her harder than the one before. She did not back away when the clothes hit her. She took every shot, was somehow relieved at the stinging on her cheeks, as if, after all, she was getting what she'd always thought she deserved.

She stood in silence, in awe, in dreamlike fear. Elliot went through the entire closet, ripped out every piece of her clothing. When he was through, he picked up her shoes and sailed them right for her head. Leah screamed and ducked and then, for the first time, understood that he hated her and ran out of the room.

He was faster and he grabbed her before she could get to the bathroom to lock herself inside. He pulled her into the kitchen, flipped on the glaring fluorescent lights, and fixed her with a stare that chilled her.

"I know you've been seeing James Arlington for three years," he said, the words straight and precise as arrows. "I know you've gone to him every Tuesday and Thursday night and screwed his brains out in his office. I know you went to him the day we got home from the cabin."

Leah slumped, and as if every word were a fist pounding on her head, she fell toward the floor. By the time he was through, she was down on her knees, crying. He stared at her, seemed to finally see her through his fury, and then pushed her away in disgust. She had to brace herself to keep from crashing into the kitchen cabinets.

"I've always known!" Elliot shouted. "You thought I was a fool, that I'd stopped looking at you. But I was always looking. Always!"

"So why didn't you do anything?" Leah shouted back up at him.

His eyes were wide, frenzied, and Leah pulled herself up. She backed into the corner of the kitchen.

"Because I loved you," he said, his anger turning to pain. He started crying, miming sounds with his mouth. Leah was both repulsed and drawn to him. She didn't know a thing about him, she realized in that instant. She had not known he was capable of shouting, of going crazy, of ransacking their bedroom. She had not known he could feel so much pain, that he must have been feeling it all along.

"Because," he went on when he could, "I thought it would pass. I thought you'd come back to me."

"I never left you," Leah said.

Elliot's head jerked up and his tears stopped abruptly. The knives sat on the counter by his hand and he pulled out a steak knife. Leah's eyes widened as he fingered the blade.

"You think I'm crazy," he said. "You think I'd hurt you."

"I don't know what to think."

He stepped toward her, smiling, the knife still in his hand. She raised her hand to her mouth, and then Elliot quickly turned and threw the knife across the room like a carnival performer. It landed in the sofa and stuck out like an extremity.

"I saw him open the door to you," Elliot said, grabbing her arm. "His fancy silk robe was hanging open. I could see him from the road. I kept thinking, 'She won't walk in. Leah would be sickened by a display like that.' But you weren't. You were eating it up."

"He makes me feel things!" Leah shouted. She was the one who was crying now. "He wants me. He's excited by me. You can't even—"

They stared at each other and, for a moment, Elliot came back to her. His face crumbled, the anger disintegrated, and she saw him, her husband. She touched his cheek.

"Oh, El, we've got to stop this."

He jerked away at her touch and stood up straight. He turned around and walked back to the bedroom. He looked at the mess in confusion, as if he couldn't remember what he had done. Then he walked to the closet, pulled out the suitcase, and opened it up on the bed.

Leah came in and stood by the door. She thought, *I'm dreaming. If anyone's going to leave, it will be me.* But as she thought this, Elliot packed his underwear and socks and shirts and pants in his suitcase and then snapped it shut.

He walked past her without a word. He set the suitcase down by the front door and then walked into the dining room. He took his briefcase off the table and walked out the door.

And don't miss these heart-stopping
romances from Bantam Books,
on sale in September:

THIEF OF HEARTS

by the nationally bestselling author

Teresa Medeiros

"Teresa Medeiros writes rare love stories
to cherish."
—*Romantic Times*

COURTING MISS HATTIE

by the highly acclaimed

Pamela Morsi

"A refreshing new voice in romance."
—*New York Times* bestselling author Jude Deveraux

VIRGIN BRIDE

by the sensational

Tamara Leigh

"Tamara Leigh writes fresh, exciting and
wonderfully sensual historical romance."
—*New York Times* bestselling author Amanda Quick

OFFICIAL RULES

To enter the sweepstakes below carefully follow all instructions found elsewhere in this offer.

The **Winners Classic** will award prizes with the following approximate maximum values: 1 Grand Prize: $26,500 (or $25,000 cash alternate); 1 First Prize: $3,000; 5 Second Prizes: $400 each; 35 Third Prizes: $100 each; 1,000 Fourth Prizes: $7.50 each. Total maximum retail value of Winners Classic Sweepstakes is $42,500. Some presentations of this sweepstakes may contain individual entry numbers corresponding to one or more of the aforementioned prize levels. To determine the Winners, individual entry numbers will first be compared with the winning numbers preselected by computer. For winning numbers not returned, prizes will be awarded in random drawings from among all eligible entries received. Prize choices may be offered at various levels. If a winner chooses an automobile prize, all license and registration fees, taxes, destination charges and, other expenses not offered herein are the responsibility of the winner. If a winner chooses a trip, travel must be complete within one year from the time the prize is awarded. Minors must be accompanied by an adult. Travel companion(s) must also sign release of liability. Trips are subject to space and departure availability. Certain black-out dates may apply.

The following applies to the sweepstakes named above:

No purchase necessary. You can also enter the sweepstakes by sending your name and address to: P.O. Box 508, Gibbstown, N.J. 08027. Mail each entry separately. Sweepstakes begins 6/1/93. Entries must be received by 12/30/94. Not responsible for lost, late, damaged, misdirected, illegible or postage due mail. Mechanically reproduced entries are not eligible. All entries become property of the sponsor and will not be returned.

Prize Selection/Validations: Selection of winners will be conducted no later than 5:00 PM on January 28, 1995, by an independent judging organization whose decisions are final. Random drawings will be held at 1211 Avenue of the Americas, New York, N.Y. 10036. Entrants need not be present to win. Odds of winning are determined by total number of entries received. Circulation of this sweepstakes is estimated not to exceed 200 million. All prizes are guaranteed to be awarded and delivered to winners. Winners will be notified by mail and may be required to complete an affidavit of eligibility and release of liability which must be returned within 14 days of date on notification or alternate winners will be selected in a random drawing. Any prize notification letter or any prize returned to a participating sponsor, Bantam Doubleday Dell Publishing Group, Inc., its participating divisions or subsidiaries, or the independent judging organization as undeliverable will be awarded to an alternate winner. Prizes are not transferable. No substitution for prizes except as offered or as may be necessary due to unavailability, in which case a prize of equal or greater value will be awarded. Prizes will be awarded approximately 90 days after the drawing. All taxes are the sole responsibility of the winners. Entry constitutes permission (except where prohibited by law) to use winners' names, hometowns, and likenesses for publicity purposes without further or other compensation. Prizes won by minors will be awarded in the name of parent or legal guardian.

Participation: Sweepstakes open to residents of the United States and Canada, except for the province of Quebec. Sweepstakes sponsored by Bantam Doubleday Dell Publishing Group, Inc., (BDD), 1540 Broadway, New York, NY 10036. Versions of this sweepstakes with different graphics and prize choices will be offered in conjunction with various solicitations or promotions by different subsidiaries and divisions of BDD. Where applicable, winners will have their choice of any prize offered at level won. Employees of BDD, its divisions, subsidiaries, advertising agencies, independent judging organization, and their immediate family members are not eligible.

Canadian residents, in order to win, must first correctly answer a time limited arithmetical skill testing question. Void in Puerto Rico, Quebec and wherever prohibited or restricted by law. Subject to all federal, state, local and provincial laws and regulations. For a list of major prize winners (available after 1/29/95). send a self-addressed, stamped envelope entirely separate from your entry to: Sweepstakes Winners, P.O. Box 517, Gibbstown, NJ 08027. Requests must be received by 12/30/94. DO NOT SEND ANY OTHER CORRESPONDENCE TO THIS P.O. BOX.

Bestselling Women's Fiction
Sandra Brown

_____	28951-9 TEXAS! LUCKY	$5.99/6.99 in Canada
_____	28990-X TEXAS! CHASE	$5.99/6.99
_____	29500-4 TEXAS! SAGE	$5.99/6.99
_____	29085-1 22 INDIGO PLACE	$5.99/6.99
_____	29783-X A WHOLE NEW LIGHT	$5.99/6.99
_____	56045-X TEMPERATURES RISING	$5.99/6.99
_____	56274-6 FANTA C	$4.99/5.99
_____	56278-9 LONG TIME COMING	$4.99/5.99

Amanda Quick

_____	28354-5 SEDUCTION	$5.99/6.99
_____	28932-2 SCANDAL	$5.99/6.99
_____	28594-7 SURRENDER	$5.99/6.99
_____	29325-7 RENDEZVOUS	$5.99/6.99
_____	29316-8 RECKLESS	$5.99/6.99
_____	29316-8 RAVISHED	$4.99/5.99
_____	29317-6 DANGEROUS	$5.99/6.99
_____	56506-0 DECEPTION	$5.99/7.50

Nora Roberts

_____	29078-9 GENUINE LIES	$5.99/6.99
_____	28578-5 PUBLIC SECRETS	$5.99/6.99
_____	26461-3 HOT ICE	$5.99/6.99
_____	26574-1 SACRED SINS	$5.99/6.99
_____	27859-2 SWEET REVENGE	$5.99/6.99
_____	27283-7 BRAZEN VIRTUE	$5.99/6.99
_____	29597-7 CARNAL INNOCENCE	$5.50/6.50
_____	29490-3 DIVINE EVIL	$5.99/6.99

Iris Johansen

_____	29871-2 LAST BRIDGE HOME	$4.50/5.50
_____	29604-3 THE GOLDEN BARBARIAN	$4.99/5.99
_____	29244-7 REAP THE WIND	$4.99/5.99
_____	29032-0 STORM WINDS	$4.99/5.99
_____	28855-5 THE WIND DANCER	$4.95/5.95
_____	29968-9 THE TIGER PRINCE	$5.50/6.50
_____	29944-1 THE MAGNIFICENT ROGUE	$5.99/6.99
_____	29945-X BELOVED SCOUNDREL	$5.99/6.99

Ask for these titles at your bookstore or use this page to order.

Please send me the books I have checked above. I am enclosing $_____ (add $2.50 to cover postage and handling). Send check or money order, no cash or C. O. D.'s please.

Mr./ Ms. _____

Address _____

City/ State/ Zip _____

Send order to: Bantam Books, Dept. FN 16, 2451 S. Wolf Road, Des Plaines, IL 60018

Please allow four to six weeks for delivery.

Prices and availability subject to change without notice.   FN 16 - 4/94